It's Me

By Kate Hickey

For MJH,

Loving and believing

Prologue

I met Ben on a Friday night. It was by chance, really. Though given the fact he lived one floor above me and we attended college with no more than four hundred freshmen, odds are it would have happened eventually. What the exact odds are, I couldn't say. Sometimes the distinction between odds and fate blur in my mind, leaving me with the impression that we collided because *someone* or *something* above thought it was a good idea at the time. This greater being was most likely on their third glass of pinot noir when it suddenly occurred to them that this was the best fucking idea in the world. *Yes. Perry and Ben. Ben and Perry.* And so it came to be.

But this particular story, my story, is not as simple as boy meets girl, boy and girl touch privates, boy and girl live happily ever after. The human existence is far more complex than that. So if it's a feel good high you're after, close the book this instant and go prance through a meadow of wildflowers. And for all the others, there are real life lessons to be learned among these pages, so let us start from the beginning.

Do not smell of alcohol in a college lecture

Friday, September 19, 2003, 8:00am

My alarm went off at eight sharp, prompting me to roll over and have to think about where I was. I stared blankly at the wall in front of me. *What happened to the window?* I closed my eyes to picture it more clearly, extending my fingers towards the glass. *The window should be right here, next to my bed, looking out over the old birch tree in our front yard. I kissed Leo Martin under that tree when I was thirteen years old. His hair was so blonde it seemed impossible. He used way too much tongue.* By the time I opened my eyes the window had vanished. So had Leo Martin. All that remained was a stark, white wall.

A lawn mower revved in the distance. I shot up from under the comforter. *Oh shit. You're at college. Leo Martin isn't feeling your tit. You have psych lecture in thirty minutes.* I looked down at the ground to see that Ali's tequila bottle had tipped over, its contents now dried on the hardwood floor. Just the sight of it made my stomach churn. Bile began to leak up from my esophagus. The taste was unbearable. Like someone farted on a lemon slice and I sucked on it. I leaned over the side of the bed and gagged. Nothing came out. I heaved again, this time with more force. Still nothing.

All I wanted was to throw up my stomach lining, eat an untoasted bagel, and feel like a million bucks by the time I took a seat in the packed auditorium. Instead, I found myself rolling off the side of the bed still wrapped in my comforter, landing with a hard thud next to that damn tequila bottle. *Two weeks out of my parents' house and this is where I'm at.*

Ali slept soundly a few feet away, blissfully unaware that morning had come and I had crawled the length of the room naked to finger through her clean underwear pile. Standing to retrieve my own pair from the top dresser drawer was out of the question. I barely had the energy to swallow, which was a shame considering every ounce of my being wanted to scream out and wake her.

After all, this was Ali's fault. It was Ali who had blackmailed me into going over to that guy's apartment last night. Though she scolded me for referring to him as *that guy*. His name was Neil. As far as I was concerned, Neil was someone's dad, not someone you voluntarily hung around with at the tender age of eighteen. She insisted it would be worth it. He was a senior and he was decent looking. She could overlook his body type because she was almost certain he had a trust fund. That was the ultimate pot of gold at the end of her rainbow. Never mind about his character, or whether he took the time to properly trim his pubes.

I told Ali I simply could not live in a world where money trumped an unkempt bush. It wasn't surprising that she didn't care to hear this. She even tried to bait me further by insisting that knowing Neil, in the intimate way one human can know another after two weeks of casual flirtation, he probably hung around with other decent people. Maybe I should be more open-minded. I could find someone for myself. But I wasn't looking for the pot of gold at the end of my rainbow. I was looking to have a little fun.

None of this mattered to Ali because Neil was into her. My choice was to either live with a depressed psychopath who was forced to shamelessly masturbate right next to me for an entire year, or accompany her to this party. I knew deep down Ali was wildly exaggerating any relationship potential with Neil, but I had seen her vibrator the day we moved in and I didn't like the idea of someone jamming that thing in and out of a hole right next to my lifeless body. I threw on some jeans for the good of the team and reluctantly tagged along.

Do not orgasm at a party

Thursday, September 18, 2003, 10:37pm

Neil's apartment was everything I imagined it to be. It was small and dark, with minimal decor beyond the Grateful Dead tapestry hanging over the entrance to his bedroom. It gave me the chills just thinking about what could be lurking on the other side. The faint smell of stale farts wafted out from the vintage couch cushions, or directly from someone's asshole.

"Someone is crop dusting the shit out of this room."

"It smells fine. You think everything smells like a fart."

"Because people fart, Ali."

"Maybe it was you."

I mumbled that it wasn't me, following after her like a puppy as we made our way to the middle of the packed living room. This was where the action was. People were grinding all over each other to an old Blackstreet song. The girls were beautiful, mature. They wore their makeup perfectly. They danced in a way that was provocative, showing off their hourglass silhouettes in tank tops and tight pants. I looked down at my old bell bottom jeans. A poor choice for my first college party. They were my mom's from the 70s. She assured me that all trends cycled around. I looked back up and sighed, crossing my arms over my chest. *Someday I'll be like those girls.*

My attention landed on a couple dry humping the shit out of each other right in the middle of the crowd. Their movements were so intense it was a miracle their crotches didn't ignite. I lifted my finger and pointed in their direction.

"Look at that!"

Ali remained distracted, desperately searching the apartment for *him*. She swatted my hand away without so much as a courtesy glance.

"Don't point. It's rude."

"Oh my god. No. No, you didn't. He is...she just...she..." I threw my arms up in disbelief, slapping them back down against my thighs. "That guy just got off! He's looking right at me and he got off in his jeans!"

"Don't flatter yourself."

"That has to feel more like a rug burn than anything else."

I waited for Ali to weigh in on this, undoubtedly scolding me for bringing more attention to the situation than necessary. But a few seconds passed. Then a minute. Then a minute more. She stayed silent on the matter. I gazed over my left shoulder to find that Ali had quietly ditched me sometime after the dry humping had concluded. My eyes frantically scanned the room. I could feel my heart rate elevating. Panic had set in. The crowd suddenly shifted against me.

"Ali?"

I turned every which way. Still no sign of her. More and more people came rushing to the dance floor the moment Blackstreet morphed into Sean Paul. I tried desperately to push my way out of the masses. *Please, God. Don't let me die here.* People were backed up all the way to the kitchen, which was empty in comparison to the rest of the apartment. The blaring fluorescent lights threatened to hold people accountable for their actions. No one was in the mood for that.

The kitchen. I just need to get to the kitchen. Fixating on those fluorescent lights kept me going even when things began to feel dire. The bleakest moment came when an unidentified person pretended to use my butt crack as a credit card machine, swiping their hand slowly all the way up along the crease of my jeans. It was as if this was the fucking apocalypse and absolutely nothing mattered anymore. Certainly not the consequences associated with caressing someone's crack without consent. And just when I thought I was out of the woods, a profusely sweating male stumbled towards me, mumbling sounds that didn't quite add up to words.

"What? I couldn't hear you! The music is so loud!"

"DO YOU WANT TO DANCE?"

He screamed it in my face, burping up puke on the word *dance*. His body swayed so far to the left that I thought he would tumble over at any second.

"Oh. No, thanks. I'm just looking for my..."

Before I could finish my sentence he projectile vomited all over the lower half of my body. I gasped in horror. He wiped his mouth and shrugged, disappearing without another word. My initial reaction was to leave. Leave the party, leave this goddamn college and never look back. My parents might lose their deposit, but who really cared? My mom was just thrilled I made it through high school without an unexpected pregnancy. My dad had zero hobbies besides measuring the alcohol lines in each and every bottle in the liquor cabinet to make sure I wasn't a degenerate. Without me, they were nothing.

But it didn't feel right. Sure, Ali had left me to die in a pile full of sexual deviants, but I had lived for a reason. She needed me to save her from herself. She needed me to save her from Neil.

Pick your battles

We are getting the hell out of here right now. I scanned the living room for Ali, spotting her almost instantly. She stood alone on the outskirts of the grinding, eyes locked on the dance floor. I followed her stare to find a short, prematurely balding guy tonguing a petite blonde. *Neil.* I pushed my hair back with forehead sweat and approached her calmly. I didn't want to appear alarmist or in any other state that might discredit my plea.

"You shouldn't have to see that. Let's get out of here. *Now.*"

Without saying a word, she sullenly turned and let me guide her out the front door. I was beyond ecstatic to breathe clean air again, loudly sighing on the first exhale to make it clear that Neil was dead to me. Ali wasn't in such a celebratory mood. She walked slowly, kicking a lone rock in her path. Her eyes stayed planted on the ground as we turned down the dirt trail that led back to the cluster of freshman dorms. I glanced at her out of the corner of my eye, unsure of what to say. I didn't want to upset her further, but I had some things I needed to get off my chest.

"Everyone in that apartment had a boner."

She stopped and looked over at me. Her eyes were heavy. She was exhausted.

"I'm not really in a place to talk about this right now, Perry. Let's just go home and go to bed."

She started up again with her pathetic shuffle routine. Neil didn't love her, and as a result she could no longer pick one foot off the ground and function like a normal human being. From now on she would just drag her feet around hopelessly so everyone would know that the first guy she met at college didn't care about her pre-med schedule. He just wanted to get laid. Go figure.

"*You* are the one who brought me here, Ali! Look where your instincts just took us. Some guy threw up all over me. Look at me! I'm covered in puke!"

I glared at her with narrowed eyes, waiting for any variation of an apology. *I'm sorry. I'm sorry a guy threw up on your mom's bell bottoms. I'm sorry you watched a guy jizz in his jeans. I'm sorry Neil was a gigantic waste of time.* Instead, she continued along her way without a sliver of acknowledgement. I rolled my eyes and threw my hands in the air.

"This is ridiculous, Ali! All of this for Neil. You should have never trusted him!"

I was yelling out now for all to hear. The public display sent her over the edge. She stormed back in my direction, emotions boiling over. Miraculously, she had regained feeling in her feet.

"And why is that?"

"Newsflash! This is fucking college. People lie and scheme and prey on the weak. You are obviously weak, therefore Neil preyed on you. Didn't you learn anything from your high school health teacher?"

"I learned how to put a condom on a cucumber."

I scoffed at her ignorance, bringing my hands to rest on my hips. "Please."

"Yeah, I did. A cucumber, Perry."

"It was a zucchini."

She inched closer, until her face was pressed up against mine. She spoke slowly, teeth grinding. "It was a *cucumber.*"

"Oh, was it? Which one is bigger?"

She threw her arms up and screamed out in frustration.

"I don't fucking care, Perry! I don't fucking care about whether it was a cucumber or a zucchini. Just like I don't fucking care about two grown adults dry humping in their spare time. Believe it or not, there's a great big world out there and not everything is about you and your fucking bullshit! I'm walking home, *ALONE*! Stay out of my sight."

"Great. Just great. I'll stay out here in the dark and see what else life has in store for me tonight. How about that? Maybe the puke will dry if I stand in one spot long enough."

She stormed off without another word. I could hear her huffing and puffing ahead of me for the entire ten minute walk back to the dorm. It was as if her whole life was crumbling around her because Neil didn't want to indulge in finger sandwiches over afternoon tea.

By the time I climbed the stairs to our second floor dorm room the drama of the night was weighing heavily on my mind. Ali was being unreasonable, that was a given. But this was a turning point. We couldn't let creeps like Neil ruin a perfectly good Thursday night. Thursday nights were my nights. I raged on Thursday nights. I wore rollerblades inside on Thursday nights. This Thursday night would be no different. I flung the door open with a new sense of purpose. *Everyone knows it was a zucchini.*

"Ali?"

I grabbed an unopened bottle of tequila from her desk and held it up. She emerged from the bedroom, pulling her sweatshirt down. I acted as enthusiastic as one could possibly act after being subjected to a bunch of bullshit.

"Who wants some tequila?"

She ignored me, walking over to her old record player and throwing on her favorite album, *Abbey Road*. I opened the bottle and poured us each a heavy-handed drink, passing one off to her as she made her way over to the couch. She took a long sip, closing her eyes and letting The Beatles fill the room with proclamations of love. Her upper body swayed to the beat. Her long, dark hair fell forward around her face. She spoke softly; her eyes remained shut.

"Doesn't this song make you want to fall in love?"

I struggled to open the window with one hand, the other holding steadfast to my drink. "No."

"The idea of being with one person for life, it's so powerful."

The tequila went down in more of a shot form than a sophisticated drink. I rested the glass on Ali's desk, lighting the remainder of a joint left over from a few nights back.

"Don't go overboard."

I sucked the life out of that thing, flicking the remnants out the window and into the bushes below. Ali rolled her eyes, lifting her head off the couch to stare at me long and hard. She simply could not envision a world where a girl wouldn't want to ride off into the sunset towards a lifetime of mediocrity with any man who would have her.

"You don't mean that."

"Ali, please. You're not in the Midwest anymore. You don't have to pretend Jesus is always listening. And if he is, he knows you aren't a virgin. Besides, if tonight is any indication, I'm not so sure there are too many people at this school to fall in love with. And that includes myself."

The second drink went down like water. I needed a third.

"Perry, take it easy on the booze."

I gulped it down in defiance, setting my glass on the floor. "I'm getting my blades. I'll be right back."

Next to my bed sat my beloved rollerblades. I got them for Christmas when I was in the seventh grade. They had seen me through good times and bad. Especially the bad. The years of braces, medieval minstrel haircuts, the time I got my period all over the chair in science class. Through the years I learned that it's nearly impossible to hold onto negativity when you're blading. You simply do not have the luxury. You must focus all your energy on not tripping over a log and launching yourself down a hill into oncoming traffic.

"Do you really think Neil was that bad?" She shouted it to me from her spot on the couch. I shuddered at the sound of his name, blading backwards into the common room to show off my skills.

"He was horrifying, and I actually didn't meet him. I only saw him from a distance."

"He seemed so nice in class."

She took a sip of her drink, desperately trying to make sense of where things went wrong. I grabbed the tequila bottle off the floor and plopped down next to her on the couch, taking a swig right from the bottle.

"And you're not pathetic. I'm sure that guy put on one hell of an act."

"I never said I was pathetic."

"Forget about Neil. Why don't you do whatever makes you happy and see how things work out?"

She leaned her head back and laughed.

"That's so juvenile, Perry. That's why you're drinking tequila from a bottle and it's exactly why you're sitting here right now with those goddamn rollerblades on. And take those jeans off already. The smell is making me ill."

I held the bottle out in front of her. She hesitated, eventually giving in. She took a conservative swig. It was not enough to make a dent, but just enough to prove she could do it. I watched as she moved off the couch and placed the bottle of tequila on the ground. She pushed up her sleeves and motioned for me to hand over the rollerblades.

"Alright then. Teach me how to be happy."

Do not tell your parents everything

Friday, September 19, 2003, 12:02pm

By noon I was beginning to feel somewhat myself again. The slight breeze that accompanied me on the walk back from class helped ease the nausea that had come and gone throughout most of the morning. It was a beautiful September day and the trees lining campus looked idyllic with the ever growing presence of red and orange hues. I pulled my phone out of the front pocket of my bag. I hadn't heard from my parents in over a week. No calls. No texts. No emails. It was as if they forgot their genitals touched in 1984, resulting in a blessed child.

I held the phone to my ear and waited. If my mom picked up she would undoubtedly ask how things were going. I wasn't sure what to say. For the most part I had always been straightforward with my parents, telling them the sordid details of some of the most regrettable situations in my life. This included the time I split my head open at age fourteen after drinking from a bottle of coconut rum. I was at my friend Lily's house and had hit my head against a decorative wooden clog her mom had on display in the living room. Instead of saying I fell, which Lily begged me to do, I told them everything down to the fact that Lily's mom left us unsupervised for an hour and nine minutes while she went upstairs with her friend, Frank.

But things were different now. They didn't need to know the intimate details of my life, nor did they care to. Not that I had a thriving social calendar filled with wild sexual escapades to rehash. Though I did make a pact with myself never to wear my hair down until it grew out past my shoulders. That could change things from here on out.

As the phone rang, I rehearsed some standard responses in my mind. *Things are great.* That was suspicious to say the least. *Things are fine. I miss you.* This option was better, still a bit shallow. *Things are okay. There are bodily fluids on your bell bottoms.* This was truthful, yet unnecessary. I decided to go with something that rode the line between options two and three. The answering machine went off just as my mom picked up.

Hi, you've reached the Walshs.

"Hello?"

"Mom? Why do you always pick up on the last possible ring?"

Please leave a message...

"Perry?"

I sighed deeply. This was an unacceptable use of time. "Yeah...I'm here."

...and we'll get back to you as soon as we can. Have a great day!

"Perry? Can you hear me?"

"I'm not calling anymore if this is going to happen."

"Happy two week anniversary, college girl! I mailed you a package with a bag of candy and some other little things. Halloween decorations. Toilet paper. Don't go crazy on the candy. Nicole from down the street came back from college last May and no one recognized her." She began to whisper. "It was horrifying."

"Yeah, great. What are you doing? You haven't called me since last week."

"Honey, we don't want to smother you. You need time to adjust and meet new people."

"Nicole from down the street once hid a hot dog in her sock, Mom. Still in the bun."

She let out an elongated gasp. It was as if someone had just informed her she only had three months left to live.

"What? No. A hot dog? In her sock of all places. How curious."

"Don't be dramatic. Anyways, what have you guys been up to without me?"

"Oh, this and that. I had the carpets steamed yesterday."

"That sounds nice." I scanned my keycard and made my way into the building.

"And we can't wait for Parents Weekend. Don't forget, it's the weekend after Columbus Day."

"I have no idea when Columbus Day is."

"So, how is everything? Do you love it? Have you made lots of friends? Tell me everything."

Ride the line.

"It's okay. Some people are weird."

"What do you mean by weird?"

26

"They just do weird things." *Ride the motherfucking line. Ridethemotherfuckingline. Ride it.* "Anyways, I'm excited to eat an entire bag of candy in my sweats tonight. Thanks for giving me something to do."

She quickly became alarmed. *Why did I say this? What did it mean? Why was I sitting alone on a Friday night? Didn't I want to meet new people? Was I a lesbian? Caroline from down the street came home one day and was a lesbian. It was okay.* I assured her that I was too tired from all of the studying to care about anything other than staying in and catching up on some sleep. And I probably was not a lesbian, though thanks for the solidarity. People don't just come home one day and decide to become a lesbian.

It was true that I needed to catch up on sleep after last night's fiasco. But as far as the studying was concerned, I was funneling all of my textbook money into a dorm wide pool that paid the residential advisor a monthly fee in exchange for beer and wine coolers. I told myself that I'd go to the library whenever I needed a book. So far I had only seen it from a distance.

Turns out you don't need to study too much in college to get by. I did learn from passing a walking tour last week that the library housed some vaguely referenced manuscripts that were quite old. No one in the group asked a single follow-up question, which was great for the student tour guide who was sweating bullets on account of the fact that he made up the whole fucking story. *Yes. There are definitely manuscripts in there. Trust me. Do not go looking for them. They are dusty. One was written by George Washington. It examines the relationship between him and his wig. Moving on to the Wildmere Building.*

The parental hopefuls were eating it up, no questions asked. I imagined their inner dialogues to have British accents. *Manuscripts! George Washington! Wigs! This place must be elite. Hear, Hear!* They stood front and center, practically drooling over some made up bullshit while their offspring quietly wondered whether they'd get laid by someone in their midst. *The answer is a hard no, people. You are all still virgins for a reason.*

Do not bleed on a stranger

I collected my package right before the mailroom closed for the night, taking my time on the walk back to the dorm. It was mild out and Steve Miller Band was flowing from an open window above. The faint smell of weed filled the air. There was an eruption of laughter from inside as I approached the building, followed by footsteps hurrying down the stairwell.

I robotically held my keycard up and pulled on the handle. The door was much lighter than I remembered it to be. *That's strange.* Within seconds it came bursting open, sending the package flying from my hands and me toppling down next to it. I landed hard on my back, uprooting a dirt cloud that swallowed my entire body. Steve Miller Band raged on in the distance. I rolled around in the dirt, moaning like a crackhead coming down from a high.

"Holy shit. It's in my eyes! My eyes are burning!"

"Take a deep breath. Let me see."

The voice was calm and steady. I felt his hands touch mine as he guided them away from my face.

"I can't feel my eyes! I don't know if I can open them!"

"Why don't you try to open them and we'll go from there."

"I can't. I can't. Holy shit, they burn!"

"Burning is good. That means you can feel them. Open them up and let me take a look."

And that's when it happened. After ever so slowly lifting my right eyelid, I met his stare for the first time. He was bent down next to me, his big brown eyes narrow with concern. His dark overgrown hair fell forward onto his forehead. Everything around us was still. I opened my left eye and looked up in awe, barely able to collect my thoughts. *He is the most beautiful person I have ever seen.* I smiled at him and he smiled back, touching a gentle hand to my shoulder.

"I don't want you to panic when I say this because you seem like a very rational person, but you have blood smeared all over your front teeth."

"What?" I touched my fingers to my mouth. Everything was wet. "Oh no...I'm missing a tooth! Am I missing a tooth?"

I smiled wide. As hideous as it probably was, I had no choice. These were my teeth we were talking about. They were perfectly aligned after four hellish years of braces. Frankly, they were the only thing I had going for me. In that moment it didn't matter how beautiful he was. This beautiful stranger was going to cancel his weekend plans and investigate my bloody mouth.

"I'm no dentist, but I think you still have them all. No, wait...wait."

He squinted, moving his head around to investigate from all angles. I brought my fingers to my face, preparing for the worst.

"Have you always been missing that tooth on the bottom? The one right in front?"

"Right here?"

He laughed, bringing his hand up to my head to pull a twig from my hair.

"I'm sorry. That was cruel. I think you just bit your lip. That's all."

"What about the back ones? Check the back ones."

He nodded sympathetically. "I promise you they are all there. Even the back ones."

He grabbed my hand in his, helping me sit up. His touch felt familiar, comforting. I blushed, suddenly overcome with embarrassment. I shifted my weight slowly back onto my feet and stood up, brushing dirt from my sweatpants. The high ponytail I hadn't touched since this morning now seemed childish. I felt like a complete fool. *He should not be seeing me like this. I need to get out of here.*

"I appear to be bleeding everywhere, so..."

It was only in that moment that I noticed her. A strikingly tall blonde was looking on from a few feet away. Her green eyes popped against her short black dress. She was probably my age, though it felt inappropriate to call her a girl. She looked much older, more put together. I felt ridiculous standing next to her. I was suddenly twelve years old again, wearing a training bra, confiding in my diary that measuring my boobs every single day was a gigantic waste of time. They weren't budging.

"I'm Ben, by the way." He stuck his hand out in my direction.

"Perry. I'm Perry." I held up my hands like I was in a police lineup. "I would shake your hand, but you should never bleed on a stranger. Not that I have something in my blood. I'm fine."

Ben laughed. The tall blonde gave him a look suggesting that to laugh about tainted blood was inappropriate. He quickly cleared his throat.

"No, you're right. Better safe than sorry." He placed his hand on her back. "This is my girlfriend, Alex."

She stepped forward, giving me a compassionate smile.

"I'm so sorry about that. Ben can be a bit of a bull sometimes."

Blood was pooling in my mouth now. I could taste hints of copper, some strawberry, which I found odd but didn't have time to explore. Ben picked the package up off the ground and extended it towards me. Our hands overlapped and I felt electric. When we finally separated, I watched as he discreetly wiped blood on the back of his pants.

"I'm in 3A if you ever need dental advice."

I laughed. *A fatal mistake.* The pooling blood began to stream from both sides of my mouth. Alex looked away. There was nothing left to say. I had to fully resign myself to the fact that my life was fucking over. Ben launched into a fake coughing fit to stop himself from laughing directly in my face. I lowered my head in defeat, turning towards the door and scanning my keycard.

"It was nice to meet you..."

Her voice trailed off. She didn't mean it. *How could she mean it?* I was a stranger who fell in love with her boyfriend and then smeared him with my wet blood. I sulked my way up the stairs. And just when I thought the world was cruel enough, Tyler from the fourth floor merrily skipped around the corner. His scream reverberated throughout the entire dorm.

"What the *hell*, Perry! You're bleeding everywhere!"

A few weeks in and Tyler was already notorious for being the resident shit stirrer. He also told me on the first night of college that he banged girls, *hard*.

Those were his exact words after no one asked. The visual still gave me nightmares. I threw my hand up in his face, refusing to stop my forward motion.

"Not now, Tyler."

He leaned against the railing, crossing his arms in front of him. He was ready to hear all about it. He needed to hear all about it. He needed to tell everyone else all about it.

"You want to talk about it?"

I paused at the top of the stairs, tilting my head back and exhaling loudly.

"Does me putting my hand to your face make it look like I want to talk about it?"

He shrugged, looking down to investigate his nail beds.

"I don't know what that was about. You tell me."

If he wanted to play this game, we could play this game. I turned back towards him, slowly creeping in his direction.

"Does the blood pouring out of my mouth make it look like I want to talk about it, Tyler?" I pointed at my head. "Does the fucking stick in my ponytail make it look like I want to talk about it?"

He squirmed in discomfort, shuffling away from me until there was nowhere left to go. He bent his upper body backward over the railing in an attempt to create space between us. I lunged towards him, listening to him squeal one last time before I stormed back in the direction of my room. He let out a sigh of relief, quickly disappearing down the stairs. Once he was a safe distance away, he found his voice again.

"Crazy bitch!"

I ran over to the railing. "Come say that to my face, Tyler! I will haunt your fucking dreams, my friend."

Ali sat on the couch flipping through the channels, cold beer in hand. She was completely oblivious to everything that had gone down in the hallway. That or she chose to block it out. The minute she saw me she sat up straight, her mouth hung open. Her eyes followed me as I walked over to my desk and placed the package down.

"What the hell happened to you?"

"I fell." I was trying to stay calm, state it as a fact. After all, it was a fact. I fell. Period.

"You have blood coming out from both sides of your mouth."

I threw my hands up. So much for calm. I had had enough of everyone's shit tonight.

"You honestly think I don't know that? For your information, I have been bleeding for several minutes. Many of those minutes in front of the best looking person I have ever laid eyes on." I rubbed my forehead with my hand. "My life is over."

"You're being a little dramatic. And you just smudged dirt on your forehead."

She sat back and continued to flip through the channels.

"Me being dramatic?" I moved to block her view of the television. "Me being dramatic? No, Ali. You know what's dramatic? You telling me you found the love of your life last night. Meanwhile, he was a complete potato with fucking dad jeans! Which, by the way, I didn't bring up earlier because you were going through a lot."

Ali threw down the remote and glared up at me. "What does that even mean? A potato? You made that up."

"Maybe I did."

"Neil's jeans were normal jeans."

"You know what. Enough. Enough! Stop saying his name! I can't take this anymore." I pointed at my mouth. "Do you see this blood? Tonight is about me."

"Please explain how that is different from any other night."

I opened the fridge and took out a beer.

"It's different because you scold me on other nights and make me believe that I'm a bad person who is reckless. Tonight you are just going to let me be me whether you like it or not because I've been through a lot."

"I never said you were a bad person. Reckless sometimes, yes."

I cracked open the can and took a long drink. The alcohol felt refreshing as it sloshed around and drowned out the taste of copper strawberries.

"Well Ali, since I am a reckless person I have no problem telling you this. Neil was also wearing a belt last night. A thick, black belt."

"And you were wearing bell bottom pants."

"Yes. Yes I was."

I walked back into the bedroom, yelling over my shoulder before slamming the door shut.

"I'm gonna go bleed to death. DO NOT check on me."

If you're into someone, talk to them

Tuesday, September 30, 2003, 3:53pm

A drop of sweat rolled from my hairline down to my eyebrow. I took a deep breath and closed my eyes, resolving not to overthink it. Ben was just a normal guy who also happened to have a perfectly chiseled jawline. But I could do this. My hair was pulled back in a mature looking bun. My teeth were all accounted for and I had even thrown on some mascara for the occasion. My palms were practically drenched by the time I held my fist up to the door and knocked.

"It's open."

The afternoon sun flooded through two west facing windows in the common room. A collection of beer cans littered the coffee table. A freshly rolled joint rested on an ashtray. From the doorway, I could see Ben's face plastered across a few pictures tacked up behind his laptop.

"Hey, it's Perry."

"Hey." His head popped out from behind the bedroom door. "I just got out of the shower. I'll be right out."

"Take your time."

He disappeared back into the bedroom. I took the opportunity to investigate his desk more thoroughly. *Ben and Alex with a Christmas tree. How original. Their prom looked lame. A puppy!* My attention shifted to an older photograph that sat framed on his desk. This one was of a young boy with his father. The father was helping the young boy hold a fishing rod. The boy's face was rather serious. He held his little hand over his father's, mimicking his every move as precisely as he could. The date on the side of the picture read July 7, 1989. *Those big brown eyes haven't changed a bit.*

"I never take anything that seriously anymore."

I was so deeply involved in imagining Ben's childhood that his present day voice was startling. He ran his hands through his wet hair, moving to stand behind me. I pointed to the picture. Its edges were weathered and bent. The color had faded a bit.

"Is that your dad?"

"Yeah." Ben picked the frame up from the desk. "He used to take my brother and me to this lake by our house all the time. We'd spend forever packing up the car and unloading it. By the time we were all set up my brother and I were so bored we'd be begging to leave. It drove him crazy."

"Do you ever go anymore?"

He placed the picture back down and walked over to grab two beers from the fridge.

"Fishing? No, never. My dad passed away a few years ago and I only went because he liked taking us."

He opened both bottles, extending one towards me.

"I'm so sorry, Ben."

"It's alright. He was sick for a long time." He motioned towards the couch. "Have a seat."

As he settled into the chair across from me I thought about all the things I had planned to say. There were the jokes I had practiced in the mirror late last night after instructing Ali to cover her ears. And then there were the serious points to show him that even though I wore sweats on a Friday night, I still could be mature. But when the moment presented itself, not one word found its way out of my mouth. It all seemed silly in comparison to him not having a dad. Five minutes in and I was out of ideas. The script had gone to shit.

"So. Tell me something good."

He placed his beer down on the coffee table. Our eyes met and I quickly diverted my attention to the floor. He made me nervous in a good way. I didn't quite know how to navigate it.

"Something good. Let's see." I took a sip of my beer and thought it over. "Well, it's actually a lot harder to get blood out of clothing than I had anticipated."

Ben laughed and shook his head. "Trust me, I feel horrible about that entire night, I do. But that's kind of a weird thing to say..."

"You should feel horrible and it's a practical thing to say. I'm about to tell you how to get the blood out."

"I'm on the edge of my seat. Don't leave me hanging." He picked up his beer and took a drink.

"If you think you're going to be in a situation involving blood, wear a garbage bag as a poncho to prevent the blood from getting on your clothing. That way, you don't have to worry about stains at all. It's genius, really."

Ben stared at me for several seconds. I became somewhat concerned that I had derailed the conversation so much so that he would suddenly fake illness just to get me out of his hair. But ever so slowly a grin spread across his face and I knew right then that he was a keeper.

"Perry. What's your last name, Perry?"

"Walsh."

"Perry Walsh. There's something different about you, Perry Walsh. I like it."

I blushed, curling my legs up under me and leaning against the side of the couch.

"And what about you, Ben? What should I know about you?"

"What do you want to know about me?"

"Tell me where you went fishing."

He moved his hands excitedly as he talked about Crystal Lake. I told him I had only been to Vermont once or twice before, but never that far north. He assured me it was beautiful. A picture perfect place where he had gone to watch the sunrise the day after he buried his dad. That lake was the only place that kept him feeling connected to the past. He wasn't one for fishing, but he could sit on the hood of his car for hours just taking in the view.

"That's really beautiful, Ben."

"What about your parents? Are they cool?"

I pictured my dad the day my parents dropped me off at college. I stood on the curb, tears streaming down my face. He rolled down his window and yelled out for all to hear. *Your mother says you're going to get your period next week. Don't forget to go to the store and get yourself one of those pad thingamajigs to stick to your underwear.* He gave me the thumbs up, speeding off without another word. Dust blew up in my face as all of the other parents continued to dutifully unpack their child's belongings. They looked horrified for me. What kind of animal does that? Leaving his only child to face the world alone with a thumbs up and some bad advice.

"They're great...great. Just normal parents." I pursed my lips together, something I always did when I was telling a lie. "Nothing really sticks out."

"Normal is good. Alex's parents are neurotic and she has a tough time with it."

"Oh yeah? That's too bad. What's the story with you guys anyways?"

Oh, her? She's no one. Just some random chick I don't even like. We've never had sex. I've never even seen her vagina up close.

"We practically grew up together." He propped his feet up on the table. "The long distance shit is hard though. Harder than I thought it would be considering we're only a few hours away."

"Mmm...I bet."

I was sorry I asked. I was bored with Alex already. In addition to the obvious fact that I had nothing to contribute to a conversation about serious relationships, I wanted to pretend she didn't exist. At least for today. At least for one hour. Luckily, we seemed to be on the same page. He finished his beer and placed it down on the table.

"Perry Walsh. Do you want to do something fun?"

"Ben, I don't know your last name. And yes. I do."

He grabbed the joint off the table and held it out in front of him. "Brown."

"What?"

"My last name. It's Brown."

"Well in that case, Benjamin Brown, let's do something fun."

"Let's get high and go to the art building. The paintings are incredible when you're baked out of your skull."

Say yes to parties

Friday, October 3, 2003, 4:46pm

I had just finished touching myself and was ready to launch into a blissful pre-dinner nap when I heard the knock at the door. In typical Thursday night fashion, last night had spiraled quickly and my insides still felt like the token banana peel stuck to the bottom of a dump truck. The orgasm helped, but really worked best when followed immediately by a restful sleep.

I could just feel myself getting worked up at the thought of one of Ali's science-loving study group friends standing on the other side of that door ruining my life. It was probably the guy who told jokes containing scientific jargon I had never heard of, laughing to himself before he could even get to the punch line. God, I hated him. *Science jokes.*

"Hey, is Perry here?"

My head shot up from the pillow at the sound of the voice.

"Yeah, she's here. She might be asleep. Let me go check."

Holy shit. I stood up and tiptoed over to the door, pressing one ear firmly against it.

"It's Ben, right?"

"Yeah, sorry. I should have introduced myself. I'm Ben. I live right upstairs. I actually think we have lecture together. Biology with Schmitt?"

"That's right. I knew you looked familiar."

She paused, most likely taken aback by Ben's smile and general good looks. I couldn't blame her. But when the pause lingered a little too long, I began to inwardly panic. *Don't you dare invite him to your boring study group.*

"I'll go check on Perry for you."

"If she's not awake it's no big deal. I just wanted to invite you guys to a party I'm having tomorrow night."

"That sounds great...I'll just go check. Be right back."

I scurried away from the door and threw the covers over my body just in time. Ali crept in and made her way over to the bed, lightly shaking me as she whispered.

"Perry. Wake up."

"Hmmm?" I rolled over and forced a yawn. "What's going on?"

"BEN is at the door. Oh my gosh, Perry, he is ridiculously good looking. I had no idea *that's* who you were talking about. I have class with him! Can you believe it? I sit a row behind him."

I threw the covers off and straightened out my hair. "Don't even think about liking him. He's mine. How do I look?"

"You look like you were just taking a nap, but in a cute way. Your pants are undone."

"Oh yeah. Thanks."

I zipped up my jeans and walked over to the bedroom door with a purpose, composing myself one last time before opening it as casually as I could.

"Ben. Hey!"

"Hey, sorry. I hope you were already awake."

He greeted me with a hug. I took in his scent as quietly as I could.

"I was awake...well kind of. I was asleep. But I'm awake now, so it's totally fine."

"Um...okay. Anyways, I just wanted to see if you and, I'm sorry I didn't catch your name."

She perked up at the attention, giggling for absolutely no reason. "Ali! My name is Ali."

"Cool. I wanted to see if you and Ali were free tomorrow night. I'm having a little get-together at my place around eight. We'll probably be there until ten, then we'll head over to the party at Bridge."

"That sounds great, Ben. We will definitely be there."

"I'll be there!"

She shouted it directly into my left ear. I hadn't realized how close her body was to mine. Her hot coffee breath, coupled with my lingering hangover, suddenly made me feel nauseous.

"We will both be there."

"We will be there." The girl was out of control. I would scold her for this later. But for now, I leaned against the doorframe for support, doing my best to force a smile.

"Sounds like we will both be there."

"Great." He cocked his head to the side. "Are you alright? You look kind of pale."

"I'm great." I closed my eyes and shrugged my shoulders. "I'm great."

"Okay, great. I will see you both tomorrow then."

"Great."

The minute the door shut I puked into the trash can next to my desk as Ali looked on in dismay. Without so much as a glance in her direction, I marched back to the bedroom for my nap. Even if it was Ben on the other side of that door, this was undeniable proof that there was no point in orgasming if you weren't going to fall directly into a glorious slumber.

Do not be a girls' girl if you don't want to be

Saturday, October 4, 2003, 7:59pm

"Are we too early? We're too early. Let's come back in twenty minutes."

I spun around and took a step towards the stairwell. Ali latched onto my shoulders and turned me back in the direction of the door, unwilling to let me give in to the nerves.

"It's eight o'clock, exactly when Ben told us to come by. Now knock."

Before my hand even made contact with the door, it swung open. An unfamiliar face stared back at us. He smiled wide but didn't say a word, just blinked several times in a row, prompting me to laugh nervously.

"Hi...we're here to see Ben."

"Who's Ben?" He leaned against the door, his expression serious.

"Um..."

"I'm just messing with you! Look at your face, you're so nervous." He pointed at me as he looked over at Ali. "She's so nervous. Poor thing. I'm Tom, Ben's roommate."

He extended his hand towards mine.

"I'm Perry. This is my roommate, Ali."

"So you're the famous Perry. Very interesting." He crossed his arms over his chest. "I hear you've been here before."

He winked at me like he knew something I didn't.

"What?"

He ignored my question, motioning for us to follow him into the apartment where a handful of people were already hanging out. Ben sat in the chair. He was talking to a guy I didn't recognize. Two girls had already planted themselves on the couch. They looked familiar, probably lived somewhere in the dorm. They were all made-up, as if they were ready to hit the club and drop it low. They certainly made no bones about the fact that they were not happy to see two new females enter the equation.

I made eye contact with Ben. He smiled and stood up to greet us, throwing his arm around my shoulder and telling Ali that he was so glad she could make it. I glanced down at the couch girls and smirked. They did not appreciate Ben's attention being redirected elsewhere. Sure, Tom was cute in a quirky sort of way, but the other guy was rather out of shape and had noticeably yellow teeth. This told me he either had a pack-a-day habit or just didn't care that he had yellow teeth. Neither scenario was appealing.

"And you." Ben pinched at my back. "I'm so glad you took time out of your napping schedule to walk up two flights of stairs."

For the next few hours we mingled with Tom, Ben, and many of the potential suitors who continued to make their way through the door. I even talked to the guy with yellow teeth. It turned out he was a senior who also happened to be Tom's brother. To me, there was no resemblance and a good chance it was a lie to get me more engaged, but who was I to judge?

By party's end, Ali had taken a particular liking to a guy named Devon. I tried to warn her any guy named Devon was bad news, but in typical Ali fashion, she wouldn't have it. I also tried to warn her that he talked to every other female in the room before seeking her out. She said I was jealous.

"Don't talk shit. You over there, all high and mighty with Ben love-pinching you. Some of us are still on the hunt."

"Ben has a girlfriend and all of us are on the hunt. Stop trying to find a husband and start with the basics."

Later that night, after many more beers and a few more parties, Ben and I walked home holding hands. It felt silly the next morning as I lay in bed reflecting on it, but in the moment it gave me serious butterflies. If it wasn't obvious already, I liked Ben. And I'm pretty sure Ben liked me, in the sort of way you can like someone while still maintaining a serious relationship. But with Alex in the picture there was nothing to figure out. At least not for now.

Ali didn't come home at all. She tried to sneak in around six in the morning, but the door slammed behind her and woke me up. Later in the day, over brunch, she told me that Devon was an asshole. They had sex and then he suggested she leave. She made sure to stay just to prove a point. He seemed to miss that point entirely, responding with, *whatever*, before rolling over and falling asleep instantaneously.

"He was such a jerk. You know, this whole college guy thing, I'm not so sure it's going to work out for me. No one wants a commitment."

"It's been a month and look who you're putting all your stock in. People named Neil and Devon. The writing's on the wall, my friend. Don't be blind."

She took a bite of her sandwich, placing it back down on the plate before grabbing for a handful of chips. "Yeah, well. I need to rethink my purpose."

Do not wear a promise ring

Saturday, October 11, 2003, 10:01am

Columbus Day Weekend. The age-old celebration of the discovery of America by a complete asshole who was lost at sea. A time when every college freshman flees campus in a desperate bid to get laid by an ex. This included Ali, who took off for Wisconsin late last night in an effort to rekindle a romance with her high school boyfriend, Steve. She had dumped him over the summer in anticipation of coming to college and finding her one true love. When that didn't pan out within one month's time she went temporarily insane and called Steve repeatedly until he weakened his stance on their split.

"Maybe he was the one all along. They say friends make the best long-term partners."

"You guys aren't even friends."

I watched as she meticulously folded a sweater and tucked it carefully into her carry-on luggage.

"I know it's hard for you to understand because you are emotionally stunted, but this is what I need to do to be happy. Please respect that."

I rolled over onto my side, propping myself up on the bed with my elbow.

"I am not emotionally stunted. I am a realist. Neil wasn't real. Steve isn't real either. You'll see."

Ali searched through the massive pile of jeans in her closet, pulling a pair from the middle and sending the others tumbling to the ground. She grunted, gathering them all in her arms and shoving them back into the closet any which way they would fit. Her flight was in one hour and she wasn't even on her way to the airport.

"You're the only one who still thinks about Neil. This isn't about Neil."

"Then tell me the truth. Is this about the promise ring?"

"No, it's not." She pointed in the direction of the door. "Leave the room. I can't have you in here distracting me right now. I need to concentrate. The car is here and I'm late."

Before I met Ali, I lived a more peaceful existence, ignorant to the fact that people my age were walking around this earth handing out rings that promised nothing and everything at the same time. It took one month of observation to learn two major facts about these rings. *Fact one: People who gave or wore a promise ring were the least likely out of the entire population to get engaged. Fact two: People who gave or wore a promise ring couldn't have sex with other people, BUT, they could go down on other people, and/or touch their breasts, and/or give them hand jobs, and/or anal.*

"You better not come back here with one of those things. Promise rings are a dead giveaway that you are a fucking moron."

She grabbed her bag off the bed and stormed past me out into the common room. I scrambled to follow after her, desperately hoping she would have a change of heart. Instead, she turned and pointed her finger directly in my face.

"Promise rings are a beautiful commitment two people make at a young age. Something you would know nothing about!"

I shook my head in disbelief, bringing my hands to rest on her shoulders.

"No, Ali. That's called an engagement ring. Promise rings are for people who want to pretend they're faithful when in reality they're just fingering the girl from their sociology class."

"Go finger yourself. My ride to the airport is here."

She pulled away from me, grabbing her coat off the chair and heading out the door. I ran into the hallway and watched her hurriedly make her way down the steps. My hands held steady to the railing. I leaned forward. She was slipping away from me. I needed to say something, anything, to bring her back.

"Don't do this, Ali! You told me his penis was pathetic. Those were your exact words." I cupped my hands around my mouth to amp up my voice. "PATHETIC PENIS!"

The door shut without another word. I slumped my body over the railing in defeat.

"Not so pathetic penis on the third floor if you want to check it out."

I looked up the stairwell in disgust. "No. You don't do that. What the fuck is wrong with you?"

I ran back to the safety of my room and slammed the door behind me, sliding down to the ground. I had to resign myself to the fact that Ali was actually going through with this. Not to mention there was a creep living on the third floor. I could deal with the creep, but at the end of the day I didn't want Ali settling for a pathetic penis like Steve.

I went to bed that night with a heavy heart. Every time I closed my eyes I pictured what a pathetic penis might look like. *Maybe it was crooked. Maybe it was thin. Maybe it was short. Really short. Oh god. Maybe it was a micropenis. What is a micropenis? Maybe his penis had been removed. Maybe it was a vagina. Steve has a vagina. Oh my god. A vagina.* I tossed and turned all night just thinking about Steve's face with a vagina for lips. I finally fell asleep around six in the morning, only to be awoken a few hours later by the sound of my phone ringing from somewhere within the bed. I felt around, picking up and bringing it to my ear without looking at the screen.

"Ali?" My voice was raspy, desperate. Like a chain smoker in need of their next cig.

"Guess who's almost there?"

"Whit?"

"We're on Cummings Street. What should we do once we get to campus?"

"Um..." I brought my hand to my forehead and closed my eyes. This was all too much for me to process right now. "Just head left after the chapel, then take the first right."

Steve's vagina lips had taken over my mind. I completely forgot who I was and what I was doing on this earth. Never mind the fact that my best friends were visiting for the weekend and I hadn't seen either of them since I left town at the end of summer. The last two months had been the longest we had spent apart since we were five years old.

"When you guys get here remind me we need to talk about someone's penis."

"Was the penis inside of you?"

"No."

"Good. I want to get drunk, not spend time at a clinic."

Consider a hand job a sexual act

Saturday, October 11, 2003, 8:46pm

Erin chugged her beer. I glanced hesitantly over at Whitney who was equally unsure of where this was headed. I was rather impressed, though left speechless by her aggressive approach to the night. I thought tonight was centered around casual conversation between friends. We'd giggle about roommates and swap freshman whore stories. Though God knows I wasn't getting laid. I hoped someone else was. Maybe we'd follow it up with a John Hughes movie of our choosing.

But Erin had other plans. Unbeknownst to us, she had purchased a ticket on the fuck me express. Her eyeliner was heavy and her halter top tight. I could see the shape of her nipples through her shirt. The sound of her beer can slamming down against the table was jolting. I looked over at the clock. Five minutes had gone by since I handed out the beers. I had taken one measly sip.

"I'm ready to take things to the next level."

"Take it easy. What kind of next level things did you have in mind?"

"I don't know."

She stood up, her shadow hovering over me.

"Erin stop it. You're creeping me out. Sit back down."

"It's Saturday night. Don't you guys party around here?"

I rolled my eyes, making it very clear I was agitated that this was even coming up in conversation.

"Like I told you several times over the phone. It's a holiday weekend. Everyone is gone."

She scoffed, placing her hands on her hips and shaking her head.

"Then why am I here?" She rubbed her midsection with her hands. "Why am I wearing this? What is the point?"

"You have no one to blame but yourself. Read the room next time."

"You saw me change into this outfit and do my makeup. You had plenty of time to stop me."

"Why don't you go down on Whitney if you're so concerned with that nasty halter top going to waste?"

"Okay, enough. The both of you." Whitney held her hands out. "Can we just drink our beers and talk like normal friends do? Fuck. That was so offensive, Perry."

"I'm sorry, Whit, but come on."

I motioned towards Erin, making my eyes as wide as they could possibly go. Whitney gave me a look that told me she agreed the halter top didn't fit properly but we should all just move on with our lives. Erin was none the wiser, grabbing another beer from the fridge and sprawling out on the floor.

"Perry, Whit said you have a penis problem. Spill it."

"It's technically not *my* problem and I don't really want to rehash it because I was just getting to a better place mentally. But I will say that my roommate is in Wisconsin having sex in exchange for jewels."

"So she's a prostitute."

This thought had surprisingly not yet crossed my mind. *Is Ali a prostitute?* I took a sip of my beer and decided if she was a prostitute it was most likely by accident.

"I don't think she meant to be, if that makes sense."

We spent the next hour analyzing Erin's recent hypersexual bender, also known as freshman orientation. During her first week in Boston she went on a spree of sleeping with three guys and one girl, all within the span of seventy-two hours. She divulged that she might have given a hand job to a bartender somewhere during that time, but couldn't quite remember the details.

"Hand jobs aren't really even that sexual if you think about it."

"They are extremely sexual. You're touching a man's genitals."

"Nope. Not sexual. Anyways, I'm now in the process of laying low. I can only have sex with one more person this semester. Then next semester I'll start with a clean slate."

I was satisfied to hear that Whitney was in a slump similar to mine, even though she had a much better excuse for it. She was attending the local state school and living at home. She couldn't hook up at her parents' house, but she couldn't stay out all night either. She did report that she made out with one potential suitor. It quickly fizzled after he burped into her mouth and it tasted like sour cream and onion flavored chips.

When it came time for me to share I casually mentioned something about going down on a guy from my freshman seminar. It seemed plausible, but not noteworthy enough to garner a follow-up question. The truth was I still hadn't seen any action, unless you counted that guy at Neil's house. And then there was the hand-holding with Ben. But that felt like a secret I needed to protect.

"Wait a minute. You mean you've still only had sex with one person?"

Erin tipped her head back and laughed. I glared in her direction.

"It's not like we're that old. Sleeping with one person by age eighteen is pretty common. Whitney has only slept with one person. I don't see you jumping all over her."

"Two." Whitney held her fingers up to drive the point home. "Two people."

Erin leaned over and touched her hand to my shoulder. I scowled hard at that hand, making it clear that it was an unwanted touch.

"And let's all be honest now that it's over. Jake shouldn't really count. He was gay."

"He wasn't gay! I dated Jake for two years. I would know if he was gay."

I turned to Whitney for backup. Her eyes were planted firmly on the ground.

"Whitney?"

She looked surprised to find herself still in the room, glancing over at me and nodding her head in agreement with something. "Jake was a great guy. A real stand-up guy."

"But do you think he was gay?"

She opened her mouth to answer when Erin cut her off.

"Fine. Jake's great. He's the greatest of all time and isn't at all gay. But you need to turn the page on that. Get out there and have some sex."

"I'm working on it."

"What do you mean *working* on it? Just choose anyone. Literally anyone who is uglier than you and happy to be there. And don't use a condom, it's so much better."

"And risk getting a sexually transmitted disease? No thanks."

"No one actually gets those."

"People get them all the time. You of all people probably have one right now. When was the last time you got checked?"

"I'm going to get checked at the end of the semester, I already told you. That's when the slate is getting wiped clean."

Do not read too deeply into your dreams

Wednesday, December 3, 2003, 7:34am

"Perry, wake up."

Ali pushed on my shoulder. I opened my eyes to find her perched on the side of my bed. Her eyes were bloodshot. It looked like she had been crying for days. I was still half asleep and disoriented. I rolled over towards her, reaching out for her hand and holding it in mine. She was fine last night when we went to bed. I had no idea what could have happened in the last six hours.

"What's the matter?"

Her lip quivered as she spoke. "Something...happened."

"Okay."

I gave her time to collect her thoughts. Mine ran wild. *Her mom is dead. Her dad is dead. Steve is dead. Her dog is dead. Her sister is dead. I am dead. I am dead?* I held my hand out in front of my face to see if it was transparent.

"What are you doing?"

"Nothing." I hid my hand under the comforter. "What's going on?"

"I woke up this morning and I was..." She leaned in close and whispered in my ear. "I had an orgasm."

I laughed, which was the wrong thing to do based on her facial expression.

"Perry, this is serious!"

"Was this your first orgasm? I don't understand. Why are you crying?"

"Because I had a dream that my middle-aged history professor was going down on me and I woke up having an orgasm. That isn't normal!"

I rolled back over and closed my eyes.

"Someone went down on you in a dream and you came. Congratulations. Join the club."

"Wake up." She slapped my arm with such aggression that I shot up.

"You aren't getting it!"

"I'm not getting it."

"Besides the obvious fact that he is married with children, I have Steve! It's not right."

"Ali." It was time to teach her the facts of life. "Your history professor didn't give you an orgasm. Your brain gave you an orgasm."

"Because I was thinking of...I can't even say his name." She threw her hands up in the air. "He's not even a cute professor, you know the kind that you actually want to have sex with. He's an overweight, balding, gray-hairing professor who is so mediocre in every way possible."

"Hairing isn't a word."

"Tell me how I'm supposed to go to his class, which is today at one o'clock by the way, and feel comfortable sitting there knowing what happened between us. I have to tell Steve."

"Nothing happened! Your body was craving an orgasm and you probably saw him yesterday in passing. Brains are stupid. They can only remember certain things."

I slid off the bed and into my slippers, moving into the common room. Ali trailed after me.

"I'm telling Steve. I don't care what you say."

"You know what else you should do?"

I turned to face her, my demeanor now serious. As predicted, she ate it right up.

"What? What should I do?"

"You should call your professor's house and tell his kids. Listen kids, daddy has a secret life."

"Fuck you."

No sixty-nining, ever

Sunday, February 22, 2004, 1:21am

We spilled out of the party and into the cold night air. The steady layering of snow threatened to mess with the buzz I had spent a majority of the night perfecting. I looked over at him. My sober self would have been nauseated by the ice collecting on his patchy, black beard. Luckily my non-sober self didn't seem to give a shit. Thoughts ran wild through my mind. *His smile is decent. Bone structure oddly small. What was his name? Adam. Nate. Adam. Matt? Everything sounds familiar. At best you have thirty minutes before sobriety. You can't hook up with Adam sober.*

Something deep within me was telling me it was all wrong. I pictured my sober self bobbing up and down in a raging sea of rum. Her arms waving frantically, trying desperately to stay afloat. Sober Me wanted to get back to shore to stop me from doing this. I was determined to keep Sober Me lost at sea for as long as possible. *Fuck you, Sober Me. I'm getting laid.*

In a couple of weeks I would be turning nineteen years old. The romanticized notion that sleeping with only one person made me some kind of moral beacon was bullshit. I just wasn't getting any. No takers. Erin was right. I needed to get out there and be more aggressive. Potential one night stands were passing me everywhere. There were literally dicks everywhere for the taking: on their way to class, at the gym, out at parties, in the dining hall. I had been ignoring all of them.

My love life had remained in a holding pattern since the day I stepped foot on campus. Unless you count the drunken night right before Christmas break when Ken from one dorm over fingered me. It was still hard for me to even wrap my mind around the fact that this had been a sexual act. His movements were so sporadic and lackluster that it felt more like a visit to the gynecologist to check for a yeast infection. We didn't even make out. I just lay there as he felt around for a bit before suddenly stopping and taking a beer out of the fridge for his forty-five second walk home.

Forget Ken. Tonight things were going to be different. I was on a mission. A sexual quest of sorts. I was bound and determined to add to the excel spreadsheet I had created earlier in the afternoon discreetly titled *Perry's Lovers (penis in vagina ONLY)!!* So far there was only one entry. Jake Bell. As I typed his name into cell B2, my mind flashed to the last time we had done it. I was straddling him, on the verge of orgasming for the first time when his dad mistakenly opened up the bedroom door. My high-pitched shriek flustered him so much that he blurted out, "I'll be downstairs when you two finish." *Finish? Finish, Mr. Bell? How the fuck am I supposed to finish now?*

The next week at school I had no choice but to end our nearly two year relationship in the parking lot after class. I calmly explained that I simply couldn't be with someone whose father had seen me completely naked, riding his first born at three o'clock on a Wednesday afternoon. Jake agreed. We hugged and that was that. I hadn't spoken to him since.

Now here I stood. Potential candidate for cell C2 to my left. As the snow turned to an icy mixture he reached for my hand, linking his fingers between mine.

"Let's go to my place."

His voice cut through the night, luring me from the memory of Jake Bell's dad.

"Sounds like a plan."

I could feel his eyes lingering over me. He was strangely unsatisfied with my answer. The intensity of his stare was so alarming that it was morphing into a lifejacket for Sober Me. Sober Me was grateful for the bone, throwing the lifejacket right on and swimming towards the waiting rescue boat. *I'm losing momentum. Look away from the creepy stare!*

"Are you avoiding eye contact with me?"

He stopped walking as he waited for my response. Sober Me was nearing the boat. The relatively tame rum waves allowed her to pull one hand up and securely grab onto the side. *Do something, Perry. Think!*

"That's insane. We totally made eye contact two minutes ago and we're making it now."

He tilted his head up towards the night sky and blew his breath out. When he looked back at me, I made sure my eyes were ready and waiting.

"That's a joke right?"

"What's a joke?"

"First of all, counting the number of times we make eye contact is weird. Second of all, you just obviously side-eyed me, which everyone knows does not count as eye contact. It's like the foreplay of eye contact."

"Being the foreplay of eye contact sounds pretty good to me."

I could see the wheels begin to turn in his mind as I worked hard to karate chop Sober Me's hand from the boat, sending her flying backwards into the choppy rum sea. It seemed to only now be occurring to him that our connection might be less than genuine, more alcohol driven than anything else. He raised one eyebrow at me.

"Do you even remember my name?"

"Yes. I do remember your name." Sober Me had two hands on the rescue boat and was climbing aboard. Didn't he realize I was multitasking? Fighting a mental battle against Sober Me all while trying to remember the random details of life, such as his name.

"So you know my name is Matt."

I grimaced at the mental image of Sober Me standing on the rescue boat as it made its way to shore. One headlight led the way through the dark and murky waters. I yelped out loud at the sight, opening my eyes to find Matt staring in disbelief.

In that moment there was nothing left to do. I threw my arms around his shoulders and kissed him good and hard. This was my last ditch effort to keep Sober Me at bay. If Sober Me made it back to shore before we made it back to his place this deal was as good as dead. There was no Cell C2. Everything was riding on this kiss. To my relief it felt good. Great, actually. Maybe I had pegged this guy all wrong. His childish bone structure and overgrown beard didn't necessarily mean we couldn't have a deeper sexual connection.

Five minutes later we pushed our way through his front door, unable to keep our hands off one another. We fumbled around in the dark before he reached for the kitchen light. The moment those overhead fluorescents switched on was the moment my world went into a tailspin. The dreamy, dark memories of seconds past practically disintegrated midair. Sober Me was approaching shore. *What the fuck do I do?* I looked over and saw a bottle of vodka sitting on the kitchen counter.

"Let's take a shot." I ripped off my jacket and threw it down on a chair.

"Really?" He motioned behind him with his thumb. "I was kind of thinking we'd take things to the bedroom."

Oh no. The rescue boat had made it to shore. Sober Me was just about to get out. I started to hyperventilate, leaning forward and resting my hands on my thighs. *Breathe. You can do this.*

"Just hurry up and pour a shot. I don't feel that great."

"Should you be taking shots of vodka if you don't feel well?"

I gave him the thumbs up. "Vodka helps. It's all good."

"I think that's called being an alcoholic, but whatever you say."

He pulled two shot glasses down from the above the sink as Sober Me waded through the water towards the beach. My breathing became quick, labored. Matt looked at me with concern.

"Are you going to puke?"

I closed my eyes and took a deep, settling breath. "I'm fine. Just hurry."

He filled my shot glass to the brim, handing it to me before pouring one for himself. I took it down quickly. The warm, comforting feeling trickled all the way down my throat. I watched the ocean storm pick up again and threaten to carry Sober Me back out into the rough waters. It was working.

"Fill it up again."

He filled my glass once more. I took the second shot down just as quickly as the first. From there everything happened so fast. Sober Me became enveloped in a series of unrelenting waves. She looked fearful as the current swept her away. Her hand was the last visible trace of her body and before long, that too had disappeared under the water.

"I did it. It's over. I did it." I whispered it, relieved that Sober Me had finally been defeated.

"Did what?"

"Nothing. I'm ready. Let's go."

We quickly became sloppy, careless. Both of us tongued the other like we hadn't seen any action in decades. He picked up my legs. I straddled him as we made our way into the bedroom. I pulled my shirt off over my head and tossed it to the side. Matt laid me down carefully on the bed, standing back to undress. I watched him intently. Button by button he went, until his entire torso was exposed.

As he unzipped his pants, my eyes adjusted to the shirtless version of him, Cell C2. *Something is wrong here.* I squinted to get a better understanding of what it was I was looking at. His chest and arms were exactly what I had expected, thin with no muscle tone visible to the human eye. It wasn't my ideal body type, but it wasn't a deal breaker either. What was really troubling was his stomach region. It appeared solidly round and was protruding a little too far for a male figure. *Was he bloated?*

"Do you have to poop?"

He pulled off his pants and threw them on the floor. "Are you kidding me?"

If I didn't know any better, I would have guessed he was four or five months pregnant.

"Matt. Come on. Your bowels must be backed up with a week's worth of shit."

He looked down at his stomach and back at me. "What the fuck are you talking about?"

I stuck my finger out and quickly touched his belly to make sure I wasn't imagining it. The skin gave slightly, but for the most part it bounced back unscathed. I held my hands up to my mouth. I was horrified.

"You seriously just poked me."

I shot up from the bed and grabbed my shirt. Sober Me rose from the dead, dragging the seaweed that confined her wrists and ankles. She was bound and determined to put an end to this shit. And for the first time all night, I realized that Sober Me and I might actually be on the same team.

"I'm sorry, Matt. I can't do this."

He reached out and touched my shoulder. "Let's sixty-nine."

"Excuse me?" Still shaken by his stomach, I could barely process this suggestion. "I'm not sixty-nining with you. That's gross."

"Why is that gross?"

"I don't know. I think it seems like it would be a lot more fluid than it actually is. You know what, no. I don't have to explain anything to you. I can't do this. I'm leaving."

As I started to walk from the bedroom back through the living room, Matt grabbed for my arm in one last desperate play.

"I'll be the one on top."

"Are you delusional? Do you honestly think I want to be lying down with a dick coming straight for my face?"

I ripped myself from his grip just as Sober Me ran to shore and scooped me up in her arms. The reunion was bittersweet. On the one hand, I had lost Cell C2, for now. On the other, Sober Me and I were back together after one hell of a rocky separation. I fled through the kitchen and into the winter night thinking that I was one lucky girl. *With our powers combined, Sober Me, no one can stop us. No one can top sixty-nine this partnership.*

Do not wish to be someone you're not

Sunday, February 22, 2004, 10:16pm

"You know it's considered socially unacceptable to poke someone's stomach, right? Especially when you're about to have sex. And I can see your armpit."

Ben pointed at the large, ill-placed rip on the side of my beloved Boston Bruins shirt. Little did he know that gaping hole had been there for years. Ever since Chris Babinski clawed at me in eighth grade gym class. He caught his fat finger right in the seam. It was a failed attempt at stopping me from leading my team to sweet victory in the capture the flag spring championship. After the game, I found him crying in a small patch of shrubs next to the school parking lot. He claimed he was looking for his missing watch, but I knew something was off. He refused to make eye contact and I saw one lone tear fall from his left eye. *Chris Babinski. What a pathetic loser.*

"Chris Babinski did it."

"What? Who's Chris Babinski?"

I sighed deeply, burying my face in a couch pillow. "Nothing. He's no one."

I had woken up this morning half convinced that last night was all just a bad dream. *People aren't really out there asking women to top sixty-nine, are they? There's no way that would have worked.* After a few minutes of all but smothering myself, I pulled my head out of the pillow to find Ben staring right at me. His lips were contorting in all types of strange ways. He was trying desperately not to laugh at my condition. He knew that laughing in this moment would take away the one shred of dignity I believed I had left, though any spectator to my life would argue that the dignity well had been dry for years. I shook my head at him. It was time to face the hard facts.

"It's hopeless."

"It's not hopeless."

I tossed the couch pillow on the floor for dramatic effect. "It's hopeless, Ben. Thank your lucky stars for Alex. It's wild out there."

"Listen, Perry."

He leaned forward, picking the pillow off the ground and holding it in his lap.

"No decent man in their right mind asks a beautiful girl to ingest his penis from midair. That's not a thing people do. That's medieval circus shit. I don't even know what to say. You could have choked. You might have died."

I curled up in the fetal position. He was right. I could have died. I should consider myself lucky that I lived to tell the horrifically mortifying tale. My eyes followed him as he stood up and made his way over to the couch. He sat at my feet, placing his hand on my back. He smiled, and with that smile everything was right with the world. Ben had that way about him, somehow making a shit storm feel like it really wasn't so bad. I could be bleeding out of both ears and he'd wipe the blood away and say I didn't need it anyway. It was probably extra. That's not to say bleeding from the ears is normal. If you take away anything from this story do not let it be medical advice.

"I just want to be normal, Ben."

Without a word he stood up from the couch and headed towards the door, turning back to face me one last time. I could tell he was lingering for a reason.

Something was on his mind. He opened his mouth, only to close it again before he said anything.

"What is it?"

His shoulders raised a bit. "I don't know."

"Just tell me. Is it awful? Does everyone know?"

"No. It's nothing like that."

"Then what? Don't torture me."

"I don't know." He tapped his fingers repeatedly on the frame, a kind of nervous tic. "I was just thinking that you wouldn't be you if you were normal, Perry. That's all. Get some sleep."

Judge a man by his khakis

Saturday, April 24, 2004, 3:25pm

Ali tugged on my arm like a tantruming child. Her timing couldn't have been worse. The 80s cover band had just lit up the stage with their rendition of Bon Jovi's "Livin' on a Prayer". The campus was electric. Imagine being six years old again, your little feet thumping down the hallway as you excitedly run towards your stocking. You're desperate to see if Santa filled it up with all sorts of candy and doodads. Your eyes widen at the magnificent sight. You did indeed make the nice list again this year. *A Christmas miracle.* Santa must have been off duty the day you farted into a plastic container and sealed it tight, leaving the stink bomb on your parents' bed for your dad to discover hours later. *A vile child*, I believe he called me.

Now imagine that you're nineteen and those candy and doodad highs come in the form of beer-induced dancing and the lead singer of a band wearing a black, spiky mullet wig. *A spring fling miracle.* Even the impending threat of a thunderstorm couldn't dampen the feeling of pure ecstasy. People were strewn out all over the main lawn living in the moment, whatever that moment meant. These were the good old days. The predawn days. The days when you could act like a complete asshole without worrying about your future boss finding an old picture of your tits floating around the internet somewhere. You would have to print out a picture of your tits and scotch tape it to your boss's forehead if you wanted to get called out.

"Come on. Let's go."

I pulled my arm away from her grip.

"Are you kidding me? The band just went on. I'm not leaving now."

"Perry, don't do this. We already talked about this."

I ignored her, choosing instead to chug the rest of my beer and scream out the lyrics along with the rest of the crowd. Ali crossed her arms over her chest and waited me out. She wanted nothing more than for me to look over in her direction so she could glare into my soul. I didn't dare give her the satisfaction.

"You're the saddest person here."

"You're not even singing the right words."

"Oh, look." I pointed up to the sky. Ali's gaze followed my finger. "That rain cloud stopped right over your head. How fitting."

"You know what? I'm leaving."

"Lighten up. We can go to boring old Ted's later."

She grabbed my face in her hand so suddenly that my compromised reflexes didn't stand a chance.

"Stop it! You're pinching my cheeks!"

"Listen to me. Ted isn't boring. You've never even met him. He's a great guy. He's having a party. It started two hours ago. I am attending and so are you because you promised and that's what friends do. They keep their promises."

I did agree to go to Ted's party when she approached me a few days back. But only because she was standing in front of the television during a late-night viewing of the Titanic. It was much easier to appease her than to argue and potentially miss Billy Zane cradle a crying child as he finagled his way onto a lifeboat. I looked longingly at the stage, moving only my eyes.

"Can we go at the end of the song?"

"No, we cannot go at the end of the song. We're going right now."

She released me and stormed off. I reluctantly dropped my cup on the lawn and followed after her. I looked back at the stage only once, when the crowd began to gain momentum for the start of "Jessie's Girl". I threw my head back and dragged my feet.

"I love this song."

"Get over it."

Ali talked excitedly about Ted for the entire ten minute walk over to his place. I learned that they met through mutual friends at a late-night pizza joint and they both preferred the same brand of orange soda. She found this to be of particular interest, considering the general population believes a different brand to be superior.

"Orange soda is gross."

"Once you get to know him I think you will love him. You guys are a lot alike."

I stopped walking in protest. "Don't do that."

"I'm not doing anything."

"Yes you are. You're trying to manipulate me into having a good time."

"I just think that you and Ted have a very similar sense of humor. That's all."

We approached a clearing at the end of the wooded path and my primal instincts took over. *You've been here before.* I closed my eyes and sniffed around. I had read somewhere that if you lost the use of one sense, the others would become magnified. I sniffed deeper hoping it would bring greater clarity to the situation. When I opened my eyes, I narrowed in on the first floor apartment to the left of the path. *Apartment number nineteen.*

"Apartment nineteen. Why is that familiar?"

"It's Neil's apartment."

I dropped to my knees and held my hands up towards the sky in a prayer position.

"Dear God. Do not let Neil be at this party. I will never be able to trust Ali ever again. Why do bad things happen to good people? Amen." I completed the sign of the cross for good measure, though God of all people knew I hadn't kneeled in a pew for years. Hopefully we were still on good terms.

And then I heard it. Almost like a lightning bolt coming down from the sky at that very moment to acknowledge my prayer. Ali laughed. *Ali laughed?* I was so caught off guard that I looked around to make sure it wasn't at someone else's expense. On any other day this same dramatic outburst would warrant a signature Ali lecture. *Perry, you are a child. Stand up. Neil is a great guy. What is the matter with you? You're such a dick sometimes.*

Upon closer examination, I realized that her hands were trembling. It dawned on me that I hadn't even questioned her relationship status with this Ted character. She had mentioned him in passing, but hadn't given any indication that he was noteworthy. There had been no talk of marriage, or even oral for that matter. Besides, she was still parading around with that phony promise ring glued to her left ring finger. This fact was now confusing yet vindicating all at the same time.

Ted's apartment was a safe distance away from Neil's, across the courtyard and up one floor. From outside we could hear Dave Matthews Band playing softly as several male voices laughed in unison. I pressed my ear against the door to investigate further.

"What are you doing? Get away from there."

Ali was whispering. She would be unable to bear it if her fuck buddy opened the door and saw her roommate crouched down attempting to gather intel.

"Shhh. Just shut up. This is the only way to know what we're walking into." I cupped my hand around my ear. "There's good news and bad news. Wait..." I closed my eyes to concentrate on a mysterious thud. "Okay, never mind. I thought I heard something else. Anyways, there's good news and bad news. Which do you want to hear first?"

Ali rolled her eyes. "The good news."

"The good news is there's probably weed in there. Which is actually great news."

I gave her the thumbs up. She motioned with her hand for me to get on with it.

"Are you ready to hear the bad news?"

"Yes, Perry. I'm ready to hear the bad news."

"The bad news is that a male just asked another male if his loafers come in taupe. I'm out of here."

She latched onto my arm to prevent me from leaving.

"You're not going anywhere. I'm knocking on the door. Get ready."

I watched as she worked to straighten out the creases in her jean shorts, something I didn't even know was possible. *Did she hear what I said?* Against my better judgement, I took a step back from the door and waited. Ali took a deep breath and moved forward, her fist about to make contact with the door.

"Wait." I threw my arm out in front of her. "Do you honestly think this is a good idea based on the information I gave you?"

She ignored me, knocking twice and continuing to nervously flatten out her shorts. After a few seconds we could hear the sound of heavy footsteps making their way towards us. When the door finally swung open, I found myself face-to-face with the man himself. Ted.

I'll admit, I was caught off guard. His blue eyes were striking against his olive skin. His sandy blonde hair had a slight wave that made him look distinguished for his age. Maybe I hadn't given Ali enough credit. My palms began to sweat. He smiled, greeting Ali with a kiss on the cheek before turning his attention to me.

"You must be Perry. I've heard so much about you."

He extended his hand towards mine. I couldn't stop staring at his crotch. His khaki shorts were incredibly tight. Ali nudged my arm. I would be lying if I said I wasn't a little disappointed that I didn't get a kiss on the cheek. But, what's fair is fair. Ali had likely earned that kiss.

"Likewise." I had never said *likewise* before in my life.

"Please, come in."

There were about a dozen males milling about. All had khaki on. Some wore khaki shorts, some wore khaki pants. Some wore cologne that choked me. Ted motioned for us to have a seat on the couch.

"What can I get you ladies to drink? Sauvignon blanc for you, Ali?"

"Perfect. Thank you."

He winked at her. It was a sexual wink. I added it to my growing list of mental notes. *Ted has given Ali a wink that implies after three glasses of white wine he will be doing her doggy style somewhere in this apartment. Probably on the bed. His golf shirt insinuates that he isn't very experimental. More to come.*

"And for you, Perry?"

"Just a beer."

"What style of beer do you prefer?"

"I like drafts. Kegs. Bottles. Cans. Surprise me."

We both smiled at him until he was safely out of sight. The minute he disappeared into the kitchen I lost my shit.

"Hi. My name's Ali. I'll have a sauvignon fucking blanc. What *is* that? I've never seen you drink sauvignon blanc, ever. Are you having sex with Ted? He is *hot*."

"Yes, we are obviously sleeping together and keep your voice down. I really like him so please, just don't bring up Steve. I still need to deal with that."

"Fuck Steve. I'll call him right now and tell him it's over."

She twisted her promise ring nervously with her fingers.

"I told Ted this ring belonged to my great-grandmother."

I threw my head in my hands. "Why would you ever say that? Now he probably thinks your great-grandmother was poor and had terrible taste."

"Well I had to say something! He asked about it."

"I love the new conniving Ali. Is this a new chapter in your life?"

"Don't say that! I'm not conniving."

She was so disgusted with this interpretation of her character that she raised her voice a bit, catching herself only when a khaki pant-wearing gentleman turned his head to see what all the commotion was about.

"Sorry! Sorry about that. She's not conniving. False alarm."

He nodded politely, quickly turning back to his conversation.

"I need to hear you say promise rings mean nothing."

"He's coming back."

"Say it."

She started laughing hysterically to drown out my voice, slapping my knee with her hand as hard as she could. "Oh Perry, that was *so* funny!"

"You ladies certainly know how to have a good time." Ted passed out the drinks, lifting his into the air for a toast. "Cheers, ladies. Thank you for joining us."

I clinked my beer bottle against Ted's glass harder than expected, causing him to raise an eyebrow. Ali extended her wine glass towards my beer. I pulled the bottle quickly to my chest. *I am not cheersing you. No way. Not until you say promise rings are shit.* Ted settled back on the couch and threw his arm around Ali. She squirmed in discomfort. I was having the time of my life watching it all unfold.

There we were, just the three of us. Ted and Ali were having sexual intercourse. I remained single, though optimistic now that I was in such close proximity to two good looking people who touched their unmentionables together in the throes of a passionate affair. Things were now complicated with Steve, but I was happy for Ali. She wasn't settling anymore. She knew she was too good for a vagina-penis and she went out and got a guy with a large bulge underneath his khaki shorts.

Ted shuffled the melting ice cubes around in his nearly empty glass, letting the last of the whiskey slide down his throat. He had this way about him that was hard to explain. When his eyes landed on me the attention was nerve-racking. In a weird way, it made me want to take my shirt off just to prove something. It was easy to see why Ali would choose to disrespect her promise ring with this guy. Of all the guys to go down on in secret, he was the one. Ted placed his glass down on the table, leaning back again before he spoke.

"So, Perry. What do you think of my shorts?"

"Um..." I was caught off guard in a good way. "I think they're great. I was just thinking about them actually."

"Oh yeah? Do these old crotch grabbers put you in the mood?"

"Ted." Ali playfully punched him in the ribs. On the outside, she was maintaining her cool. On the inside, I knew she was mortified. She swiftly took down the rest of her wine.

"I think they are tight in all the right places."

"See Ali. Just like I told you. Everyone likes to see what they're getting themselves into."

He winked at me and from that moment on I knew. Regardless of what happened with Ali, Ted would be in my life forever.

Do not show your boobs to a Dick

Sunday, September 5, 2004, 7:55pm

Ben broke up with Alex the first weekend of our sophomore year. He confided in Tom and me that it had gone *almost* exactly as expected. She cried and told him he was a dick. He asked if they could still be friends. She shoved him out the door and slammed it shut behind him. By the time he made it out to the parking lot, his duffel bag had been ceremoniously launched out of her third story window, its contents littered across the concrete. Then came the grand finale, the unexpected twist. She opened the window and yelled down to the street that she had shown her boobs to her neighbor, Richard, just last week. And he liked them.

"Showing your boobs to someone is kind of a weird thing to do as a solo act."

"Wait a minute." Tom sat back on the couch. "She called you a dick *while* letting a Dick look at her breasts? Seems a bit hypocritical to me."

Ben finished his beer, crushing the can and tossing it into the trash. "Tell me about it."

"Well, this is great news, man. We can finally have some fucking fun around here."

"Tom, come on. My relationship had nothing to do with us having fun."

"I wasn't having fun when Alex told me to pick up my socks."

"She didn't do that."

"Oh, right. Just like she didn't forbid me from eating the cheese at late-night snacks because she claimed I had dairy bloat. I still have no fucking idea what dairy bloat is by the way, and I don't appreciate it."

"Whatever. It doesn't matter anymore."

"I'm just saying. You were too young for that shit, dude. That's like some, *I have two kids and a mortgage to think about,* shit. We should be worrying about nineteen-year-old shit."

"Oh yeah, like what?"

"Like eating out the senior in my biology class who licks her lips every time she looks at me. It's crazy. Sometimes she throws in a wink. But not all the time. She likes to keep me guessing."

Tom rested his head on the back of the couch and closed his eyes. A smile spread across his face. The image he was conjuring up was something I wanted no part of.

"That's my cue. Sounds like you guys have a busy night ahead of you."

Ben walked me to the door, following me out into the stairwell.

"Believe it or not I actually missed your face over the summer, Perry Walsh."

"This face is a very missable face, Benjamin Brown."

"You sure you don't want to stick around?"

"And ruin your first night out as a single man? I don't think so."

Tom threw me the peace sign from his chair. "Later, Perry. I'll let you know how it all plays out. You had first dibs. Just remember that."

Ben laughed, lowering his voice so only he and I could hear. "That is true. You have first dibs. You know that. We could eliminate Tom altogether. It could be fun."

"How romantic." I started down the stairs. "As tempting as it is, I think I'll pass. Enjoy your freedom."

On the walk back to my place I had to bite my lower lip to keep myself from smiling. I didn't want anyone to see me from afar and start spreading the word that I was talking to myself. I wasn't established enough at this school to rise above that kind of reputation.

Ben was single and there were now question marks hovering around our relationship status. I didn't want to get my hopes up, but for the first time in a long time I was excited at the prospect of what could be. I also had a growing suspicion that fate had intervened and left me a college virgin for a reason. Which was nothing short of a miracle, considering that the last weekend of freshman year I got down on both knees and pleaded with the decent spirits above to clean the dust out of my pipes. I then ran mad through the dorm asking any living male if he would like to have sex with me. Most thought it was a joke and laughed it off. *Hilarious, Perry. Good one.* Others were straight up afraid. No one agreed to it.

Have sex with someone you actually like

Thursday, September 23, 2004, 11:23pm

Ben pushed me up against his door. Our make out session was becoming so intense that it took someone commenting, "Yeah. Get it," on their trip down the stairs for us to realize we had not yet made it into the privacy of his apartment. He fumbled with the keys, dropping them on the ground before hurriedly scooping them back up to unlock the door.

We started up again without so much as turning on a light. A year's worth of growing attraction had led to this moment. He sat on the couch and I straddled him, pulling my shirt up over my head. Our kissing became more urgent.

"Wait."

He ran to the bedroom and came back with a condom. Somewhere along the way he had ditched all of his clothing. I shimmied out of my underwear and tossed it to the side, straddling him again and wrapping my arms around his neck. He moved my legs, spreading them apart and pulling me forward. One of my bra straps slid down the side of my arm.

I moved my body up and back down again until he was in me for the first time. He leaned his head back against the couch, grabbing my butt in his hands. A soft moan escaped from my lips. I rode him for a long time in the darkness of his living room. He kissed my chest and neck, eventually pulling my bra off. We were both breathing heavily. *Holy shit. This is so much better than Jake Bell.* Our movements became faster and faster, our bodies increasingly in sync.

"Oh my god."

"I'm almost there. Fuck. Let me get on top."

We flipped positions. I lay my head down against the couch pillow and he pulled forward. He moved with slow, purposeful motions until it was inevitable. I screamed out at such a high volume that anyone within a mile radius was now involved in our first sexual encounter. I didn't necessarily categorize myself as a screamer until that cry poured out from the depths of my soul. This orgasm was undoubtedly more intense than any that were self-inflicted. For the first time in my life another human being had gotten me off, no thanks to Mr. Bell. Ben wasn't far behind.

We drifted off to sleep that night to the steady hum of the window fan in his bedroom. The sheets felt cool against my bare back. When the sun came up we did it again. This time under the privacy of his comforter. The second time was somehow better than the first and I thought this was definitely something I could get used to.

Do not let fear rule your mind

Saturday, October 16, 2004, 10:45pm

Ali grabbed my hand as we navigated our way through the crowded house party. She led me past the couple making out in the stairwell and into the kitchen where a freshly poured beer sat on the countertop. The lumberjack manning the keg nodded to Ali that it was hers for the taking. I'm not usually one to trust any old drink sitting around in the presence of a giant male wearing a cut-off flannel tank top, but I decided to let this one slide. Ali had a lot on her mind tonight and I had seen this guy once or twice around campus. He seemed harmless enough.

"Your tits look amazing in that shirt, Ali."

Flannel shirt guy raised his eyebrow. *Like you've never heard the word tits before, guy. Relax.* Ali was noticeably tense. Her jaw was clenched so tightly you could practically see her teeth grinding through her skin. She took a deep breath and gave me the look signaling that it was time. She grabbed her beer and disappeared back into the crowd in search of Ted.

Tonight was make or break for them. Things had been a bit rocky since she overheard him asking a girl with a black lace thong sticking out over the top of her low-rise jeans if she had ever experimented with food items in bed. He told Ali that he was asking for a friend, something she tried desperately to believe. I could hear her lying awake at night, repeating it over and over to herself. Almost like some fucked up form of self-brainwashing. By the third night, I found myself wondering if I should intervene. I even went so far as to call my mom and ask what the definition of a cult was according to the dictionary. *I think a cult has to have more than two members. Check on it for me just in case, will you? Get back to me.*

On night four Ali woke me up a little after three in the morning to confide that she couldn't carry the burden any longer. She knew deep down Ted wasn't asking for a friend. In fact, he had once asked Ali the same exact question. *Signature Ted,* she called it. I told Ali that I had been trying to stay out of it based on her alarmingly fragile mental state, but who the fuck asks a girl to shove a corndog up her vagina for a friend? Ali clarified that it was much more of a chocolate syrup situation. Not something as violating as a corndog. *No food actually goes inside of your vagina.* I rubbed her back for a few minutes more, silently fixating on whether it was appropriate to ask for more details. *So, did you do it? Did you smear chocolate syrup all over your tits?* Ali further clarified that it was a good time to shut the fuck up about the logistics.

I leaned back against the kitchen counter now and waited patiently as Paul Bunyan poured me a beer. We made eye contact and I smiled. He chose not to reciprocate the sentiment, something I found odd, considering I was obviously way out of his league. I sighed loudly, which also went unacknowledged. *I guess he's into dudes.*

Things were officially complicated with Ben. A few nights after we had sex I dreamt that he came over to my apartment to tell me he was back with Alex. In the dream he also went into incredible detail about his orgasm while they were in the reverse cowgirl position. Then he stood up and walked away.

I reached my hand out to stop him. He slipped through my fingers. I reached out again. I couldn't get to him. I yelled out in desperation, but he couldn't hear me. Before I knew it, he had vanished without a trace. I woke up in a panic. My sheets were drenched in sweat. I decided right then and there that the best course of action was to play it cool. The dream had served as a warning. I couldn't smother him or he'd run right back into her waiting arms. I had to play it *cool*.

But playing it cool was out of my emotional realm, so I turned to the next best option. Avoidance. It was hard to do, but not impossible. The dining hall was where things got tricky. I knew Ben usually went to dinner around six, so I made sure Ali and I were there promptly at five every night. We were to be in and out of there in forty-five minutes. There was no room for error.

A few weeks into our routine, Ali arrived home late to prove some sort of point about acting like an adult. By the time we sat down it was 6:15pm. *Prime time.* I spotted Ben almost instantly. He was sitting with Tom and a handful of other guys two tables

116

away. I panicked and told Ali I would call her parents and tell them I saw her snorting a line if she didn't shove that fucking pork fried rice down her throat. *Shovel it in there, let's go. We need to get the hell out of here.* Ali told me that her parents would never believe she was doing coke and that I was fucked up in the head. *Emotionally stunted*, as she always liked to say. *Ben likes you. You like Ben. Let things happen naturally.*

"Earth to anyone. Do you want the beer or not?"

Paul Bunyan's voice was more feminine than expected. His breath reeked of cigarettes.

"What?" I took the beer from his hand. "Right, thanks."

"You alright?"

"Yeah. I'm fine." I motioned in the direction of his shirt. "Interesting concept. A flannel shirt as a tank top. Kind of defeats the purpose."

He looked down at his shirt. "I made it."

"You sewed it?"

"I cut the sleeves off."

"Cool."

"It keeps my core warm."

"Gotta keep the core warm."

He smiled at this and I felt accomplished. Like I had changed him from a cold-hearted villain to a lovable giant. He really was just an oversized teddy bear in need of some hugs.

"Do you live here?"

"No. They just hire me to work the keg."

I laughed a little too loudly, playfully punching him in the shoulder. Ali once told me that the key to flirtation was maintaining physical contact. He looked down at the spot I had touched then back up at me.

"You just punched me."

"Sorry. I'm sorry. It was supposed to be playful."

I brushed his shoulder as if this would undo the damage. He gently pushed my hand away and moved over in the opposite direction, burying his face in his cup.

"Don't mind her. This is her first beer ever."

His voice cut through the awkward moment and made my blood freeze. Paul Bunyan was none the wiser, shrugging his shoulders and heading off towards the front door.

"Whatever. I'm going to have a cig."

I turned to find Ben leaning up against the wall, his right hand in his pocket. He motioned in the direction of the door with his drink.

"He seems like a good catch."

"Once you get to know him he's a really lovable guy."

He laughed and shook his head. His eyes stayed steady on me. He appeared to be contemplating something. Probably something to do with us having sex and then not speaking for almost a month.

"What am I going to do with you, Perry Walsh?"

He pushed himself off the wall and made his way over to where I was standing. My heart was beating so rapidly I was convinced it would pop out of my body at any moment.

"You punched him, by the way. Did you know that?"

"I was creating physical contact. Guys like that."

"Did you read that in your *Cosmopolitan*?"

"Ali told me."

"Well, if Ali told you then it must be true. Where have you been by the way? Have you been avoiding me?"

I wanted to jump into his arms and tell him I was a complete asshole. Ask him to forgive me for being awkward and insecure over a dream. He would whisk me away from this old, sticky kitchen; from Paul's cigarette breath and Ted's food fetish. But I couldn't find the right words. It was hard to be truthful when the moment called for it.

"I've just been really busy, that's all."

"Well are you busy now?"

There was no denying the chemistry between us. My mind wandered back to that dream. The thought of Ben slipping through my fingers and running back to Alex. I wouldn't let it happen. Things would be different this time. I would be honest and mature about my feelings. I parted my lips to let the words out.

"No. I'm not busy now."

That night I let things happen naturally. I didn't overthink it. I didn't agonize over how things could eventually dissolve and leave me in shambles. That night we did the reverse cowgirl exactly as I read about in my *Cosmopolitan*. Afterwards, I lay awake in his arms thinking I shouldn't think so much.

Find someone who makes you laugh

Tuesday, November 9, 2004, 6:14pm

Ben and I walked from his apartment clear across campus to the student union, debating the entire way if Tom had engaged in a threesome one night earlier.

"There were three voices. I know there were. And he's always talking about threesomes. The guy is on a mission."

"It could have been one girl changing the depth of her voice for some sort of role play."

Ben considered this, opening the door as I made my way inside.

"Alright, say that's true and it was one girl changing her voice. Explain why there weren't four voices."

We walked down the hallway, past the mailboxes and towards the pub.

"I don't get it."

His hands were animated now. He was passionate about cracking this case.

"How come Tom wasn't role playing with his voice?"

He did have a point. Based on everything we could hear standing in our underwear, ears shamelessly pressed up against the shared wall, there was no denying the facts. Three people went to bed in that room last night. Or, three people had a weird sexual encounter with meditation music playing softly in the background and then went their separate ways before going to bed. We ordered our dinner and took a seat in a booth by the door.

"What did you get?"

"Chicken caesar wrap."

He stuck his tongue out like he was going to gag.

"It's good! And I got chips. Salt and vinegar."

"I got a personal pizza. You can't have any."

"I don't want any."

"There was never a choice."

I laughed, leaning back against the booth. The pub was relatively busy for a Tuesday night. I scanned the room and locked eyes with someone familiar. She scowled and it activated my memory. It was one of the clubbing couch girls from Ben's party freshman year. She was scarfing down nachos with her couch friend. Ben followed my eyes to her table, smiling and waving once he recognized who it was. She blushed, waving back before quickly diverting her attention back to her friend.

"It's Angie." He turned back towards me. "Remember Angie from our dorm?"

"Of course I remember. She's in love with you."

"What?" He turned to look at her. Their eyes met for a second time, prompting her to nervously smile, pick up her tray, and scamper off. Her friend followed quickly after her. They had a lot to talk about, I was sure of it. Ben turned back to me none the wiser. "She is not *in love* with me. She's my friend. She's really nice."

"She practically had to leave because you made eye contact with her. She's probably rushing back to her apartment to change her underwear."

"Oh my god, Perry. Come on."

"It's the truth."

He slurped up the last of his soda, coming up for air with a smile.

"You're so jealous of Angie."

Our numbers got called from the kitchen and we stood up to grab our trays.

"I'm not jealous of Angie, I'm just stating the obvious. She's in love with you. I don't blame her. I can see the appeal."

"Well that's too bad for her."

We sat back down. I went directly for the bag of chips.

"Oh yeah, why is that?"

"Because I'm with you."

I took down an entire chip in one bite trying to process this information. It scratched the side of my throat, sending me into a coughing fit.

"Are you okay?"

I took a drink of water, returning the cup to the table.

"I'm fine, sorry. Something went down the wrong way." I leaned in close and whispered. "Are we together?"

"Yeah, I would call this together." He pointed back and forth between us. "Why are you whispering?"

"What does together mean exactly?"

He practically inhaled an entire piece of pizza before answering.

"I don't know. We're together. I like you. You like me. I don't want to sleep with other people. Do you?"

"Not really."

"That's a questionable response. *Not really*."

He grabbed a napkin and requested a pen.

"I don't carry a pen around."

"Then in your mind check yes if you like me, check no if you don't like me, and we'll go from there. It's not that complicated."

"Okay." I closed my eyes and pretended to mentally check yes or no. When I opened them again he was staring, waiting for my answer. I reached for my chips without a word.

"And?"

"You'll never know."

"You obviously checked yes. Everyone here knows you checked yes."

"Maybe. You'll have to wait and see."

"Angie would have checked yes."

He devoured the rest of his pizza. By the time I got back to my apartment that night, our conversation still felt surreal. Just like *that* we were together. Ben and I were an actual thing. It seemed easy. Too easy. Maybe too good to be true. One thing was certain. Angie definitely would have checked yes. But then again, so did I.

Do not make out with anyone from your art history class

Sunday, December 12, 2004, 7:35pm

"So let me get this straight. You went to a party last night and made out with who?"

I took a long, slow sip of my beer. The memory of our make out session tortured my brain. There was not one bone in my body that was attracted to him. I was drunk and being overly sexual. He was decent in the moment. Before I knew it, he had me up against the wall of the bathroom where some other stuff might have happened too. But in the version I wanted to relay to Ben it was strictly kissing. Nothing more. He may not have forgiven me otherwise.

"He's just this freshman, James. He's in my art history class. We were talking and the next thing I knew we were making out. It meant nothing. I was super drunk."

He laughed awkwardly, looking away to collect his thoughts.

"You can't just." He turned his eyes back on me. "That's such a copout, Perry. What if I went out tonight and made out with someone? Would it be okay tomorrow if I told you I was *super* drunk?"

I would be devastated. Just the thought of it rocked me to the core. He and I had been seeing each other for almost two months. I couldn't get enough of him. But for the sake of my defense, I couldn't let him know that. I had to play it off.

"It's not that big of a deal, Ben. Things happen."

He nodded his head slowly as he took this in.

"So what is it we're doing here, Perry?"

Don't say it. You don't mean it. You'll regret it.

I shrugged my shoulders. "We're just having fun."

"That's great."

He stood up and walked over to the window, placing his hands on his hips.

"Well how about this. I'm not having fun anymore." He turned around to face me. "This isn't fun for me. I think you should leave."

"Fine."

I stood up, begging any higher power above not to let this be happening. To give me the courage to say something. *I didn't mean it. I'm falling for you. James sucks. Art history sucks. It was all a mistake.* But in usual Perry fashion, nothing came out. I shut the door behind me, tears streaming down my face.

Anyone claiming to have a perfect life is full of shit

Saturday, March 12, 2005, 4:43pm

"Ben and I have something I can't explain. I can't even put it into words."

Alex's long blonde hair fell delicately around her perfectly made-up face. When she smiled, her nose scrunched and I could see soft laugh lines forming around her eyes. She would age gracefully, I was sure of it. But aging gracefully didn't matter right now because all I could think about was the fact that she showed her boobs to some guy named Richard.

"It's this crazy, cosmic connection."

"Wow, that's..." I was stuttering. "Cosmic though?"

"I'm really into astrology."

I chugged the rest of my beer. When the bottle was empty I placed it down on the concrete step, scanning the festive St. Patrick's Day crowd for anyone who looked remotely familiar. I finally made eye contact with Dan who sat a few rows behind me in sociology.

I only knew him because he somehow managed to have a coughing fit during every class. My professor would have to stop and address it to make sure he was going to live. This prompted me to glare at him until he felt shamed. It wasn't so surprising that my S.O.S. wave was met with a dirty look and the cold shoulder. *Fuck you, Dan. Fuck your coughs too.*

"What about you, Perry?"

"Hmm, what? What about me?"

"I don't know." She ran her fingers through her hair. "I've known you for what, almost two years. I've never heard Ben mention you having a serious boyfriend or anything like that."

Oh, there was one guy. I was falling for him. He was falling for me. We saw each other naked and it was incredible. Then I made out with regular old James and he went back to having a totally cosmic connection with you and my life is in utter ruins. But thanks for asking.

I shrugged, crossing my arms and resting them on my knees. "I guess I just haven't found the right person. We're twenty years old. It's not the end of the world."

"No, I get it. Not everyone finds their soulmate at age fourteen."

I gagged. It wasn't intentional. It was my body's primal reaction to Alex's interpretation of her life.

"Are you alright?"

"I'm fine. I'm going to get a refill. Do you need anything?"

"No, thanks. But if you see Ben, tell him I'm looking for him."

I spotted Ali sitting on the couch in the living room next to Lance, her most recent love interest. She met Lance at a party last weekend. *Seven days ago.* Within one hour of meeting, he told her that she had soulful eyes and from that moment on, she knew. He was the one for her. I was once again left disappointed by her naivety.

I told Ali that Lance was way too serious for my liking. He didn't understand sarcasm, and he wasn't nearly as funny as Ted. I missed Ted. And Lance wore his pants too high. Her only defense was that Lance hadn't yet propositioned her into making ice cream sundaes out of her breasts.

"What's up, Lance?"

Ali sprung off the couch and practically jumped on top of me, kissing my cheek repeatedly. She looked like a baby kangaroo trying to climb into my front pouch.

"Perry! Where the hell have you been?"

I stuck my hand out to high five Lance. He was hesitant, but knew the consequences would be too steep. He stuck his hand out and I slapped it with mine.

"You got her nice and drunk. Someone's getting laid tonight."

He tilted his head to the side. "I would never try to get a woman drunk to violate her."

I pushed Ali off me and clapped my hands together.

"Alright kids, listen up. Enough with your nasty hookup details."

Ali sat back down next to Lance, cuddling up to his shoulder.

"I hope you two have been having the time of your fucking lives in here because I've been outside with Alex, where she just informed me that Ben is her cosmic lover."

"Is that a Cher song? Cosmic lover. That sounds like a Cher song."

"I know Lance, right?"

Maybe I just needed to warm up to him.

"Oh please, Perry. You deserve it. You had your chance." She turned to Lance and whispered loudly. "Don't feel sorry for her. She deserves it."

"I can hear you. And yes, I made one mistake. I'm a human being."

"Cosmic love is a serious term, Perry. People don't just throw that around for no reason."

"Lance." I pinched the bridge of my nose between my thumb and index finger. "I was just starting to like you, Lance."

Have sex in a costume at least once

Saturday, October 29, 2005, 9:12pm

"Who wants a jello shot?"

I held up two paper cups and scanned the sparsely decorated apartment for any takers. No one flinched. No one even looked over in my direction. Everyone just continued on with their dull conversations as if there wasn't a sexy lion standing in their midst. I took one shot down quickly and stared at the other. *What the hell?* I took it down and tossed the empty cups in the trash. It was like it never even happened.

I searched the crowd for Ali, spotting her in the middle of the living room dancing wildly with a few girls I recognized from our freshman dorm. She was dressed as a slutty doll. A terrifying smile was hand-painted across her cheeks with eyeliner. It didn't translate well to sexy. I danced up to the group. A girl whose name I couldn't quite remember cheered and grabbed my hand. I leaned in close to Ali.

"You are stealing the innocence of childhood with that costume."

She cupped her hand around her ear. The music blared so loudly that it was nearly impossible to have a conversation.

"I said, you are scaring the children! I don't think dolls have tits!"

"Your raccoon costume isn't much better!"

I looked down at my costume. It did come off rather raccoon-like with the pointy ears and the heavy black eye makeup I had added for dramatic effect. But it was one of the only costumes left in the store and the woman at the cash register said it looked perfect on me. She might have used the word stunning. Besides, it was either this lion costume or the homemade Edward Scissorhands idea I had been toying around with for the past week. A few days ago I had gone so far as to duct tape several pairs of rusty scissors to my hands before deciding it just wasn't sustainable for a college party. They were heavy and I couldn't pick up a beer.

"I spent sixty dollars on this costume. It better look like a fucking lion."

"Don't look now but I think Shrek is checking you out."

I glanced over my shoulder to find Shrek awkwardly walking like an Egyptian to the beat of the music. He was attempting to lure me in with his stare. I would not be lured. *Stop it. I will not be lured. Turn away.*

"God no."

I moved to the other side of the group and safely out of his sight.

"We've got another live one. Darth Vader is approaching."

I felt a hand on my shoulder and some sort of plastic material against my neck.

"You are unwise to lower your defenses!"

"Can we help you Darth?"

He pulled up his mask, revealing a familiar face. "Perry! It's me, Darren!"

"Oh my god, Darren! You were so believable!"

He bowed, satisfied with his performance.

"You play a great Darth Vader."

"I've been wanting to use that line on someone all night."

Darren and I met a month prior when we were assigned a partner project in history class. I thought he was cute until he opened his mouth and talked endlessly about the inner workings of his boring long-distance relationship. He was from Iowa and his high school sweetheart attended a university near their hometown. He was a nice enough guy, a little too literal and way too serious about love. But nevertheless, he was doable.

"I thought you were visiting Jill this weekend?"

Darren leaned in and yell-talked into my ear.

"Jill has a ton of studying to do. So I decided to back off and let her concentrate on her work. She's going to be a doctor. Did I tell you that?"

Studying on Halloween weekend always equals banging someone else. Poor Darren. So innocent. So oblivious.

"A doctor. Great. Anyways, I have just the thing for you."

I dragged him over to the refrigerator and picked up two shots, one red and one blue.

"Red or blue?"

"My favorite color is green."

I shook my head. He was so helpless, like a newborn baby or a good retriever puppy.

"Nope. Red or blue."

He shrugged and grabbed the red shot out of my hand.

"What should we toast to?"

I lifted my tiny plastic cup to his.

"To Jill. The hardest working woman I know. I can't wait to spend my forever with her."

"That's not really what I had in mind, but fuck it."

The jello slid down my throat just as my favorite song came on over the speakers. Every female in the room let out a simultaneous cheer and reminded the person standing right next to them that this was *their* song. I was not above it.

"I fucking love this song!"

I jumped up and down and squealed in Darren's face. He nodded in agreement.

"It's a great song. A real party starter."

"Come on, let's dance!"

I grabbed two more jello shots and handed one to him. He put both hands up in protest.

"Oh, no. I really shouldn't. I try not to have more than one drink a night. Jill says too much alcohol is unbecoming."

"Darren, it's fucking jello. And look, this one is green! It's your favorite color. It's a sign!"

He smiled and gave in, reaching his hand out to grab it. "Sure, why not. It's Halloween."

"That's what I've been saying this whole time! Oh my god. We're totally in sync. Nothing matters on Halloween!"

The dance floor was packed with sexy variations of anything you could possibly imagine grinding up against characters such as those from a galaxy far away. I grabbed Darren's hands in mine and threw them up in the air, attempting to wow him with my sexiest dip to the ground. From my perspective it felt flawless. I was dropping it like it was hot. From an outsider's perspective it most likely looked as though I had squatted down to take a poop in a city sewer. I stood back up and threw my ass into his crotch, pulling his arms around my waist. He promptly removed his hands from my body and backed away.

"Whoa...I can't do this."

"Do what? We're just dancing. It's not that big of a deal."

He looked like he wanted to run away and curl up to a picture of Jill while an acoustic guitar played softly in the background. I moved closer to him and whispered in his ear.

"I won't tell Jill. I promise."

What I really should have said was, *Jill is out fucking someone right now you idiot. She doesn't give two shits about what you're doing.*

Darren looked down at the floor and shook his head. "I can't."

He disappeared into the kitchen without another word. *Whatever.* The dance floor was hopping and I was going to have a good time regardless of what Darren from Iowa was up to. "Hollaback Girl" turned "Gold Digger" turned "Candy Shop" and I noticed Darren lingering around the kitchen doorway, more jello shots in hand.

After a while, he finally mustered up the courage to approach the dance floor again. Without a word he started grinding up behind me with an awkward bending of his knees. I grabbed his hips in my hands and we danced for a few more songs until we were both sweaty and solidly drunk. I turned and threw my arms around his shoulders. He leaned in and yelled into my ear.

"Want to get out of here?"

He kept his Darth Vader mask on for the entire five minute walk to his place. It was an unnecessary attempt to hide his identity. I tried to tell him no one cared or even knew that he had a girlfriend. Most people didn't even know who the hell he was, or that he even went to our school. He would not budge on this.

Once we were within the safe confines of his apartment, however, everything changed. Darren's lame personality quickly morphed into a strange, hypersexual alter ego. He tossed his mask carelessly on the ground, grabbing me around the waist and pushing me up against a wall.

"I've been wanting to do this since the first day I met you."

He began to kiss my neck. I looked on in surprise.

"Really? I was under the impression that we didn't have anything in common."

He stopped and stared at me intently. After a few seconds of lingering silence he laughed loudly, his breath smacking me in the face. I laughed nervously right back at him, not sure what it was we were even laughing about.

"You're funny, Perry. I like that about you."

He grabbed my hand and led me over to his bedroom. A plaid comforter was tucked neatly into his perfectly made bed. His dresser and nightstand were littered with cheesy pictures of him and Jill participating in various couples activities. I walked over to the dresser and picked up one of the frames, pointing at it in disbelief.

"Did this moment really happen organically? Who took this picture?"

Darren and Jill were holding ice cream cones. He had chocolate; she had vanilla. They both pressed their ice cream onto the other's nose and laughed like it was the best fucking decision in the world. He grabbed the picture out of my hand and threw it face down.

"My mom took it."

He reached for my hand and led me over to the bed.

"What was your mom even doing there?"

"Forget about the picture."

His lips pressed against mine and I went with it. The kiss was soft and slow at first. We sat awkwardly at the foot of his bed. After a few minutes it began to get more intense. Darren laid me back and within minutes we were full on groping each other. I began to pull up his Darth Vader costume. He quickly grabbed my wrists and held them down.

"Wait..." He kissed me a bit more before he finished his thought. "I was thinking we would leave our costumes on."

"You want to have sex with a black sheet on?"

"It's not a sheet. It's a cape."

I looked away for a moment and pondered this, thinking it wasn't the strangest request I'd ever heard. At least neither of us was still wearing a mask that would have made it slightly offensive.

He pulled a condom out of his drawer. I flicked my thong over to the corner and thought about taking the paw booties off my feet, ultimately deciding against it. These paw booties were a necessary component of the costume. Darren climbed back on top of me and began to speak in a serious tone.

"Are you ready for this you dirty, filthy lion?"

Surprised by his significant change in personality, but rather into it, I tried my best to keep a straight face.

"I'm ready."

With his body weight on top of me, Darren lunged forward. He was breathing heavy. I grabbed onto his back.

"You like that?"

"I like it."

We began kissing again, his movements more rough.

"I'm going to give it to you, you *fluffy* lion."

"What?" My voice was breathy. "Say something else."

"I said fierce. You *fierce* lion. Do you want it?"

The volume of his voice was getting louder.

"I think so."

This was getting a little complicated. The headboard of his bed began to rattle against the wall.

"Oh, you filthy, lion. Filthy, dirty lion."

I tried to get into the game.

"You're a dirty Vader."

He came to an abrupt halt, holding still as he looked down at me.

"You can't just say Vader without the Darth. You have to say Darth then Vader right after it. Darth Vader. That's my name."

"Sorry."

"And Darth Vader isn't dirty. Use words like powerful, dangerous, daddy. Daddy is a good one. Father. What not. Something like that. Something sexy and mysterious or with the daddy undertone."

"Sexy and mysterious daddy. Got it."

I grabbed onto his biceps and held on as we started up again. After a few minutes I gave the dirty talk another try.

"You're so dangerous. Oh, daddy. Give it to me."

He leaned in and whispered in my ear, "How dangerous?"

"So dangerous."

"Who's your father?"

"Nope. Not going there."

I was out of breath and officially creeped out, but we were both on the verge. I wasn't about to waste a perfectly good orgasm just because he fucked up. He spoke louder and with more authority.

"How dangerous?"

"So dangerous!"

After we finished, Darren decided it was a good idea to rest his sweaty head on my chest. I closed my eyes and pushed my hair back away from my face. The countdown could now officially commence. I had come to find that waiting a full five minutes before fleeing the scene of sex was ideal, especially after the first time. Any amount of time shorter was cruel, any longer unnecessary. Darren closed his eyes. I stared at his digital clock, eagerly counting down my wait.

At 2:54am time was up. I yawned and stretched my arms dramatically over my head. He didn't move. I sat up, pushing his body off of me. He fell limp onto the side of the bed. I looked around for my thong. It rested on a stuffed animal frog. I turned to face Darren, struggling to stretch the thong over my lion booties. He lay completely still in his black sheet. Without the mask he kind of resembled a dead priest.

"Alright. Well, that was fun. I'm glad we did that."

Darren opened his eyes and propped himself up on his elbows.

"You aren't staying?"

"Oh, no. I want to sleep in my own bed."

"But we just had sex."

I waited for him to finish his sentence. When I realized that was the end of his thought I felt rather bad. *He really is clueless.*

"We did have sex, Darren, and it was fun. But you have Jill and I think the alcohol is going to wear off within the next hour. We should be apart when that happens."

I walked towards the bedroom door. Darren threw himself back down and sighed deeply.

"You're right."

I made it halfway through the living room before I heard *it*. The slight whimpering noise. *Don't turn around. Don't indulge him.*

"I just..."

The whimpering continued. I rolled my eyes and slowly turned back to face him. I didn't dare get any closer, addressing him from the safety of the living room.

"What was that?"

He was curled up in the fetal position. It was disturbingly feminine. I had just had sex with someone who could readily find themselves curled up like a teenaged girl with menstrual cramps. This was not the dirty talking, dangerous man I had let inside of me five minutes ago. I covered my eyes with my hand and shook my head.

"Please don't lie like that."

He sat up and made his way towards me. I held my hand out in an attempt to stop his forward motion.

"You don't need to come any closer. Please. Just stay where you are."

"I'm sorry. I just feel like...I feel like you're so awesome. But I have Jill." He paused dramatically, his hands resting on his hips. "She's my soulmate, Perry. But now you and I have something. Can you be in love with two people at the same time?"

"No, you certainly cannot. And for the record, we are not in love. We had sex. Meaningless sex. You are going to stay with Jill and we are going to pretend like this never happened. That's how this is going to go down."

I stormed over to the front door.

"Wait."

He ran up to me, resting his hand against the door in protest of my leaving. He lunged forward and jammed his tongue down my throat in one last-ditch effort to rekindle our love. I pushed him off of me with so much force that he stumbled backward, nearly falling to the ground.

"Stop it. That was disgusting."

"I'll never forget you, Perry."

"We have class together on Monday."

I threw open the door and hightailed it out of there. *That's it. Tomorrow I am making a cup of tea, buying a notebook, and sitting down to map out where the fuck my life went wrong.*

Do not announce your business in a public setting

"I'll have a large coffee, please. Black."

I pulled a few crumpled dollar bills from the pocket of my sweatpants. The student barista grabbed a paper cup and filled it slowly.

"And then what happened?"

Another cafe employee stood leaning against a broom. She would not sweep for a second longer. Not until she heard every detail of the intensely personal account of what went down last night.

"He was probably inside of me for like, five seconds until he came."

She pushed the lid down on my cup and slid it across the counter.

"Will that be all for you today?"

"Yes."

"And then he thinks he's going to text me to come over again tonight? As if I'm some blow up doll he keeps around just for the hole. What has he done for me lately? I can't get off in five seconds."

"You are so much more than just a hole, Christina. He's the hole."

I tried not to picture anyone's hole as she rang the coffee up and handed me the change. I dropped a few quarters in the tip jar and thanked her, turning to find that a decent line had formed since I had stepped up to the register. Everyone waiting had gone the way of horrified stare or stifled laughter. There was no in-between. Except for him. He was second from the end and looking right at me. He lifted his hand and waved. I smiled back at him, a pang of nostalgia washing over me.

"Fancy seeing you here."

"Wait for me. It won't take that long. Probably only five seconds."

I laughed, making my way over to the top of the stairs. I leaned over the railing and looked down on the first floor. It had been a long time since we had talked. I had seen him around campus here and there, but we hadn't exchanged more than a friendly hello since that day one year ago when he told me things weren't fun for him anymore. It had been painful to say the least. Especially since he ran right back to *her*. But time has this way about moving people along. Eventually you heal or become completely numb. I'm still not sure there's a difference.

"Sweatpants kind of night, huh?"

I looked down to see that we were both wearing gray sweats topped off with mismatched sweatshirts. I reached out and tugged playfully on his jacket.

"I like the way you accessorized yours with this peacock. Very classy."

He laughed as we walked down the stairs. "It's called a peacoat, Perry. Not a peacock."

He pushed the door open and held it for me as I passed through. Once outside, I turned towards him. He was looking at me in a way that felt good. The way the old Ben used to look at me before things got messy. I missed him. There were so many things I wanted to say. I looked down at the icy pavement, about to open my mouth when I heard him speak.

"It's good to see you, Perry."

I smiled up at him, nodding my head in agreement.

"It is really good to see you, Ben."

"Are you doing anything tonight?"

"Um..." My eyes became shifty. I was nervous. "No. Well. I'm supposed to be studying for finals. But you know how that goes."

"Come over? We can watch a movie. Wait, let me think." He squinted, trying to recall which Christmas classic was my favorite. "*Home Alone*."

"That's right."

"See, I remembered."

"You're pretty smooth, Benjamin Brown, but everyone likes *Home Alone*."

"What do you say, Perry Walsh?"

"I say, yes."

We huddled close together and watched the McCallisters take off for Paris. I was safely tucked under his arm. Snow began to fall outside of the window. My head rested on his chest and as the credits rolled, he gently played with my hair, tucking it behind my ear. I looked up at him and smiled. Without saying a word he leaned down and kissed me. It was a soft, innocent kiss. We lingered in it for several seconds before he pulled away. His eyes were still closed when he spoke.

"Is this bad?"

I leaned in and kissed him again. This time the kiss was deeper, more intimate. Things quickly intensified. There was a fleeting moment where I considered the potential of this ending poorly. We had just gone a year without talking and yet here we were again, detaching our brains from our bodies because who really cared about emotional well-being in the heat of the moment? I pulled my lips away from his.

"Sorry. Too much?"

I knew he was with Alex. I knew Ali wouldn't have the patience to listen to the bullshit all over again. But I didn't care. I wanted Ben and I wanted him tonight. As far as I was concerned, tomorrow was a hundred years away.

"No. I was just thinking we should move into your bedroom in case Tom comes home."

"Good idea."

He playfully carried me back to his room, tripping on an old sneaker along the way and nearly sending both of us careening into the wall. We laughed as he laid me down on his bed, whispering again that he missed me. Our bodies fell into old habits. It was as if no time had passed.

The next morning I rolled over to see that Ben was already awake. He smiled, pushing my hair back away from my face and kissing my forehead. I excused myself, climbing out of bed and making my way to the bathroom. I turned on the sink, splashing cold water on my face. When I looked in the mirror, uncertainty stared back. I wanted to be optimistic, but I honestly didn't know what I was.

Do not talk in a library

Tuesday, February 7, 2006, 2:45pm

I sat across the table from him, furiously scanning the screen of my laptop for the psychology paper that was due tomorrow. If this paper went missing there was no way I could replicate the entire thing in one night. It had graphs, quotes, and studies that involved samples of friends - most of whom I had spent hours making up.

"Shit. I can't find it."

"Maybe you saved it to a file."

"What does that even mean, *saved it to a file*? That makes no sense."

Ben played with his pen, clicking the bottom over and over again.

"Stop doing that."

"Doing what?"

"Clicking your pen."

A guy sitting at the table next to us aggressively shushed in our direction. Ben leaned forward and whispered.

"See, now you've upset that guy."

"Oh my god, wait...is this it?" I opened a file titled *Mustache Rides.* "I called it Mustache Rides. Why would I do that?"

"You were probably drunk and in need of a mustache ride."

"There's no way I did that. Maybe Ali was messing with me."

"So...now that this whole mustache ride crisis has been averted, is this a good time to tell you that I slept with someone?"

I had just attached the document to an email when he blurted it out. *He slept with someone?* In all the time I had known Ben Brown he had been with Alex or me. Me or Alex. It was one or the other, certainly not some new unidentified person. I peeked slowly over the top of my laptop. His facial expression was serious. This was not some sort of bad joke to get me riled up.

"You slept with someone."

"Yeah. This girl Brooke. She's a sophomore. She's in my government class."

"Brooke. A sophomore in your government class. Got it."

Ben called me right after the New Year to tell me he had broken up with Alex. *This is it*, he had said. I was a bit skeptical, more relieved than anything else. I knew their connection wasn't cosmic. Ours was. And now he knew it too. We had talked every day since that night at his place. We were also sleeping together on a regular basis. When we fell into the habit, it became almost impossible to keep our hands off of each other. *Was hooking up with Brooke really worth it?* I didn't have the answer, and that ate away at me.

But it would be wrong to sit here and spew a bunch of bullshit about how horrible he was for doing this. Ben had asked me a week earlier if I could picture us in a serious relationship. *I don't know. Maybe.* That was my answer. My feelings for him were stronger than ever, don't get me wrong. I needed him in a way I had never needed anyone before. But that didn't mean I could see myself as someone's girlfriend. There would always be another James from art history and that's just the truth about growing up. I knew he felt the same way. Still, sleeping with Brooke before we had a chance to iron out the details of our relationship status caught me completely off guard. The door to our relationship had been slammed in my fucking face. For that, I was furious.

I buried my face in my laptop and pretended to concentrate on something, anything. I reopened the *Mustache Ride* file for good measure. He moved his face to the side of my computer. I kept my eyes locked on the screen.

"It just happened, Perry."

"Cool. I'm really happy for you guys."

"There's nothing to be happy about. We're just having fun."

I slammed my laptop shut and stood up, reaching for my jacket. This was exactly why I never came to the library. It was a dark, quiet place where people could drop emotional bombs on other people and the person receiving the emotional bomb was not allowed to react.

"Perry, sit down. Can we talk about this like two adults?"

I pushed my arms through the sleeves and zipped up as quickly as I could. Being an adult in this moment meant not screaming out that Ben was a fucking whore in front of all of these innocent bystanders.

"There is nothing to say. Brooke sounds lovely. Have a great life with the sophomore from government class."

I must have inadvertently raised my voice around, *have a great life,* because the guy at the table next to us started up again with his shushing. I spun around in a rage.

"Shut the fuck up with the shushes! I will shove that fucking shush finger up your ass!"

Ben brought his hand to his forehead, mouthing to the shush guy that he was sorry. I stormed out of the library thinking I was such a fool. This was exactly why I couldn't be honest with Ben. This was exactly why I would remain emotionally stunted forever, because Ben slept with someone from government class and then sided with the shush guy.

Experiment with your sexuality

Saturday, September 23, 2006, 1:34am

I stood staring at her topless chest. She had great tits. The best I had ever seen. They were perfectly round and symmetrical. Not like mine. Mine were more lopsided and you could barely grasp a handful if you tried. Hopefully she wouldn't care. She knew this was nothing serious. I wasn't into girls. This was more of a test run. To make sure I really, really wasn't into girls.

I had known Lex since freshman year. She was in a friend group that sometimes overlapped with mine. Tonight I saw her out at a party and we exchanged the usual pleasantries before going our separate ways. Later in the night we made eye contact from across the room and something felt different. I got a strange tingling in my privates. I looked away and shrugged it off. I hadn't had sex in a few months; everyone gave me a tingling in my privates. As the party ended, Lex approached me and asked if she could walk me home. I said yes and the next thing I knew we were aggressively making out in the bushes outside of her apartment complex.

Now here I stood, staring with my mouth open as she bent down and removed her underwear. I was still fully clothed and a little in shock. She approached me, reaching out and grabbing my hand in hers.

"Is this your first time with a girl?"

I nodded that it was, suddenly feeling very aware that there was a naked female in front of me. Lex leaned forward and began to kiss me, her lips parting mine with her tongue. I don't know if it was the alcohol or something more, but in that moment there was an attraction between us that was real. We continued to kiss as she played with the bottom of my shirt, pulling it up over my head.

"Let's go into the bedroom."

She led me back to her room. All at once I was overcome by the fact that I was about to get with another female and had absolutely no idea what to do. Making out was one thing, but what about all the other stuff. I didn't want to disappoint her.

"I've never done this before."

She shut the door and spoke matter-of-factly.

"Don't worry. I'll lead."

We began kissing again. Lex pushed me back onto the bed and climbed on top of me, rubbing her entire body against mine. She unbuttoned my jeans and pulled them to my ankles, moving my underwear to the side as she slid her fingers into me. I pulled my face away from hers and made a strange noise. Almost like the sound a dog would make if its foot got run over by a car. *Oh no. Was that a bark?* She stopped, looking down at me to see what was the matter.

"What's wrong?"

"I don't know. I'm just not used to this."

"Don't overthink it. We're all humans."

We're all humans? Undeniably true. I lay back down and we started up again. But my mind would not relax. *What happens next? Are we going to scissor? Do I go down on her? Is her clitoris in the same place as mine?* I pulled back suddenly.

"What do we do next?"

She hung her head and sighed.

"Why don't you just let things happen naturally? Is this how you are with guys?"

"With guys I know what happens next."

"It's really not that different."

She climbed off of me, plopping down on the other side of the bed.

"Why don't you try going down on me?"

This wasn't really what I had in mind. But I guess it couldn't be *all* about me. I maneuvered myself into a position at the end of the bed and sat staring at her vagina.

"I've never seen a vagina up close."

"You do know you have a vagina, right?"

"Is there some sort of method or do I just start licking?"

Lex propped herself up on her elbows, she was becoming impatient with my antics.

"Are you fucking kidding me, Perry?"

"I don't know, okay! I don't fucking know."

"What usually happens when a guy goes down on you?"

I shrugged, thinking I never asked a guy what he was doing down there. He could be digging for gold for all I cared.

"I don't know. They move their tongue around for a while until I've had enough and then we have sex."

She lay back down, covering her eyes with her hands. "This was a bad idea."

I threw myself down next to her. "I'm sorry. I'm an amateur."

"You're an idiot."

"Thanks for fingering me and stuff."

She laughed, standing up to throw on some sweats.

"And I like the design you have there." I pointed at her pubic region. "It's kind of like an arrow leading to your vagina."

"It's called a landing strip."

I stood up and zipped my pants. She pulled down her shirt, resting her hands on my shoulders to shoot me straight.

"And Perry?"

"Yeah?"

"Do yourself a favor. Go home and look at your vagina in the fucking mirror, will you?"

Be in tune with your body

Sunday, September 24, 2006, 2:02pm

He parked the car next to a tree a few blocks down from the art building. We passed a joint between us, listening to The Cranberries on the local radio station.

"Ben?"

"Yeah."

"Can I ask you a question?"

"Of course."

I took a long hit, watching the end of the joint as it lit up evenly on all sides.

"When you go down on a girl, what do you do?"

He threw his head back against the seat and laughed.

"Is this a joke?"

"No, it's not a joke. I'm being serious. I want to know. Do you have a move or are you just winging it?"

He rolled his head to face me.

"For starters, that's insulting because I've gone down on you many times. Obviously it wasn't that memorable."

"It was breathtaking. But seriously, do you have a plan when you do it or do you just kind of go with the flow?"

"I use pretty much the same strategy on everyone."

"Thanks for making a girl feel special."

"There has to be a plan, Perry."

I shrugged my shoulders. "I don't know if I would notice the difference between a plan and no plan."

"You don't think you'd notice the difference between a plan and aimless nonsense?"

"No, I don't."

I passed the joint back to him. He took one more quick hit, tapping it out on a quarter and starting the car.

"I thought we were going to look at art."

He pulled out of the space and started down the road.

"The art can wait. We are going to test out this theory."

Only buy drugs from a trusted source

Thursday, May 3, 2007, 12:36pm

"What do you mean you gave us placebos?"

Tom stared at Jimmy. His expression was blank. It was obvious he wasn't comprehending why the hell Jimmy would be carrying around sugar pills or how, as an amateur drug dealer, he didn't know the difference between a sugar pill and the real deal.

"Alright, it's like this." Jimmy was anxious, shifty, most likely high on the supply he meant to sell to Tom. "You know the other day in the library? I told you guys I had some pills that you could use to study for finals? Well, somehow I mixed up those pills with the sugar pills and I gave you the sugar pills."

"But why do you even have sugar pills? That's what I'm not getting."

"Relax, Tom. Backup."

Tom threw his arms up in the air. "I'm perfectly relaxed."

"I carry around a lot of things that aren't your damn business."

"I want my twenty bucks back, dude."

Jimmy sped off on his bicycle without another word, leaving us in the dust and Tom out twenty bucks. After the confusion had settled a bit, we continued our walk to the dining hall. It was grilled cheese day, the best day of them all.

"Was that interaction real or did I dream it?"

"It seemed real. But I didn't touch him or anything so I can't be sure."

"You know what'll be nice in the real world?"

"What's that?"

"Drug dealers having their shit together."

"I know. They're probably so much more professional."

"They have to be. It's their livelihood."

The dining hall was packed. I grabbed a tray and power-walked over to the hot food line.

"It's grilled cheese day, motherfucker!"

We waited for over ten minutes to get our hands on those precious sandwiches. Tom begged for two. The female server must have been feeling his vibe because she agreed to it, even after she had just finished giving me the dreaded speech. *If I give an extra to you, then I'll have to give one to everyone. Then what? Then there's no grilled cheeses.* Tom promised to split his extra with me on account of him feeding me Jimmy's sugar pills.

"So. I heard you and Jane broke up."

Tom sighed, holding his grilled cheese in his hands. "I totally fucked up, man."

"I'm sorry, buddy. What happened?"

"Well." He took a bite of the grilled cheese, throwing it back down on the plate in defeat. "I got shitfaced and banged the girl who lives below us. She's a temptress that one. It was only a matter of time. Then I ratted myself out and sobbed on Jane's lap for three hours until she forced me to leave her place. It was pathetic."

"I'm sorry, Tom. We've all been there."

"Yeah, I guess."

He picked the grilled cheese back up and wolfed it down, divvying up the second and placing half on my tray.

"Anyways, what's up with you? I haven't seen you around in months so you're not screwing Ben. He dumped Brooke. Did you know that? It was savage. I think he still carries a torch for you. Just saying."

"Stop it."

"Tell me everything. What's going on in the love department?"

"Department is closed."

"Come on. It can't be that bad."

I sat back and closed my eyes to recount the events that had gone down during this academic calendar.

"Let's see. I made out with a freshman before he threw up on my bare chest. I had sex with someone whose name I still don't know. I can only recognize him sometimes, when his hair is blowing in the right direction. I was fingered by a girl, a hot girl. Oh, and I let a foreign exchange student go down on me. Ben and I did some stuff here and there, but that doesn't really count."

Tom shook his head in disbelief, wiping his greasy hands on his napkin.

"Straight up, I would trade my academic calendar hookups with yours in a heartbeat. I want a foreign exchange student to go down on me. That's so cool, Perry."

"It sounds cool in theory. But male foreign exchange students are not as desirable as female foreign exchange students. This one definitely wasn't at least."

"It sounds to me like you've knocked it out of the park. Well done."

"It can only get better from here. That's what I keep telling myself."

"Not necessarily, kid. I hear it can be rough out there. People try to be serious and settle down and shit. Take my advice. Let as many foreign exchange students as possible go down on you over the next few weeks. Girls and guys."

Do not listen to a career advisor

Friday, May 11, 2007, 12:02pm

After months of prodding from my parents, I decided to pay a visit to the career center as most dutiful seniors do. Dutiful seniors being those who cave to the barrage of harassing emails and lectures about life in the real world being tough. *Don't make it any harder on yourself,* they warn us. *Stop by the career center and have a student volunteer inform you that your resume is shit unless you add a line at the bottom notifying your prospective employer that your weekend interests include hiking, trying new restaurants, and using a puppy as a pillow to recover from getting blackout drunk and puking up duck sauce all over your couch.*

Attempting to navigate a resume with zero life experience was tough enough, never mind the fact that employees from the campus health center simultaneously began stuffing each and every mailbox with pamphlets. Endless amounts of pamphlets. These pamphlets informed the graduating class that all of us probably, most likely, definitely had a sexually transmitted disease. They couldn't be sure, but probably we did. We shouldn't panic. The good news was that we could all head over to the health center and get a full check on our parents' dime. But we better act fast, because once we were in the real world we would still most certainly have a sexually transmitted disease, but our copays would lead us to financial ruin.

I lay awake at night, my mind consumed with fear. I couldn't wrap my head around the fact that people wanted to live in the real world. A frightening place where jobless, hopeless individuals ran around rubbing their tainted genitals together. The burden was all too much. *A copay? How am I going to afford a copay?* I thrashed around in the early morning hours, pamphlet headlines running rampant through my vulnerable mind. *Do you want to be a failure? Silent STDs: The Facts. What career is right for you? Abstinence: The Only Way to Stay Clean. Do you want to be a fucking failure with an STD? Because that's what you are. That's all you'll ever be.*

After one particularly sleepless night, I marched myself right over to the health center. I waited patiently on the steps for twenty minutes until the doors opened. Days later, I found out I was STD free, a shocking relief. The tragic news surprisingly came from the career center, where a career advisor held out no hope that I would one day become a writer. In fact, the look on his face suggested I would have a far better chance of becoming a wizard.

"So. What you're saying is, I can't move to Manhattan and write for a magazine?"

"Depends on what magazine." He tossed my resume down on the desk. "Do I see *Vogue* in your future? No. *Good Housekeeping*? Maybe in thirty years. Do I think a smaller niche market? Potentially. Perhaps one with a religious affiliation. They're dying for new talent."

"What kind of religious writing is there to do?"

He scoffed, making it very clear I was just not getting it. I was not on his level.

"Oh, I don't know. Have you ever heard of something called the Bible?" He laughed to himself, straightening out the tie he borrowed from his dad.

"It's the most published book in the world, by the way."

"I'm confused. You're telling me that editing the Bible is going to be more attainable than writing an article for *Good Housekeeping*?"

"No, of course not. No one actually edits the Bible." He held his hands out in front of his face like a mime. "For you I'm picturing small weekly items. Like the Sunday bulletin for example."

"I don't know. I'm not really that religious."

"I think it would be a great start for you. Get your foot in the door."

He leaned back in his chair, crossing one leg over the other. His fingers tapped together as he pondered whether he was going to add mayonnaise or mustard to his ham sandwich at lunch.

"That doesn't really sound like something I'd enjoy."

He shrugged, quickly becoming impatient.

"Beggars can't be choosers, now can they?"

I pushed the resume back towards him. I wasn't ready to throw in the towel just yet.

"I got an A minus on my final paper in sociology class. I think I can do better than the Sunday bulletin."

"Have you ever considered a career as a secretary?"

"I can show you the sociology paper if you want."

"I'm good." He looked down at his imaginary watch. "Oh, look at that. Two minutes past twelve. Time for lunch."

Bring water to graduation

Saturday, May 26, 2007, 10:02am

I marched in the processional with the rest of the class of 2007, hungover as fuck. We were like ants, draped in our black caps and gowns, mindlessly trudging towards the colony. Baking in the unrelenting sun the entire way. *I worked my ass off for four years and this is what I get in return?*

I spotted my extended family congregated by a tree. My younger cousin was either sleeping or completely dead on the ground. It was hard to tell. No one was tending to him, which was a good sign. I made eye contact with my mom, who took that as her cue to start cry-jogging next to me for the next few minutes, all while trying to get the perfect shot with her camera.

"Smile, sweetie! It's your day! Look at me! Look this way! Chin down. I love you!"

I did my best to smile through the raging headache that held my skull hostage. My uncle did me no favors by cupping his hands around his mouth and yelling at the top of his lungs in his thick Boston accent.

"It ain't ova' 'til you get the diploma!"

I motioned for my mom to get control of the situation. My uncle laughed to himself, elbowing my dad repeatedly in the gut. I continued onward, desperately trying to ignore his voice. But the voice was so piercing that I could still hear him by the time I made it to my chair.

"Get a load of that guy's hair piece. Who knew Thomas Jefferson was gonna be the keynote speakah?" *Shut up. Shut up. Shut up. SHUT. UP.*

Last night had gotten a bit out of control, culminating in my favorite pair of winter boots and my wooden desk chair getting tossed into a raging bonfire. I was completely shitfaced and had nodded in agreement when my neighbor preached about materialistic items being the devil's work. I woke up with a dry mouth, pounding headache, and a singed desk chair that my parents would probably have to pay five hundred dollars to replace. *First real world lesson: never trust someone who isn't practicing what they preach.*

For the next three hours, we sat still while every single classmate, their major, their hobbies, and their favorite sexual positions were announced over the loudspeaker. At my most desperate point, I placed my hands together in prayer and pleaded with the great spirits above to let me get through the ceremony without passing out. When a sudden wave of nausea pulsed through my body, I instinctively grabbed onto the guy next to me.

"Oh shit. I'm gonna puke!"

He looked over with a mixture of concern and annoyance at the fact that I was clawing at his chest.

"I can't swallow." I turned to face him, barely clinging to life. "What do I do?"

"Calm the fuck down. Have some of my water."

He reached down and handed me an unopened bottle of water he had been stashing under his seat. I stared in disbelief, looking first at the water, then back up at him, and then back down at the water.

"Are you kidding me? You've had this water the whole fucking time?"

"Yeah, I know. So inconsiderate to bring water for myself and not the asshole next to me. I'm about to graduate magna cum laude, bitch! Shut the fuck up!"

"You're the bitch, bitch!" With that, I opened the water and emptied it, letting a majority of it splash all over my gown. "This water is *so* refreshing."

"Real mature. Good luck in the real world. I'm sure you'll do great."

One of our classmates rambled about flying from the nest as our feud continued on.

"I wish I could fly away from *you*! Come at me. I dare you."

"Don't touch me!"

"You're touching me!"

"Move your knee, *right* now."

"You move it."

He turned his back on me. Twenty minutes later the ceremony had finally concluded and I puked my brains out in the privacy of a bush outside of my old freshman dorm. *Life really does come full circle.*

Later that day, as the sun began to set behind the tall pines that surrounded our small apartment, my dad and I stood staring at the remnants of the bonfire.

He lectured me on the importance of taking responsibility for my actions.

"Life is not a joke, Perry. You need to start growing up and taking things seriously. Actions have consequences in the real world. You can't just go around dumping chairs into fires."

"I know, Dad." I reached my arms around him and gave him a hug, hoping to garner an ounce of sympathy. "I made a mistake."

He kissed me on the forehead. "You're very convincing, but I'm still forwarding you the bill."

Do not bottle your emotions

Saturday, May 26, 2007, 7:56pm

I walked out the back door and down the tree-lined path that led to Ben's apartment. The gravity of the day was finally starting to hit me. My hangover had dissipated and its absence left room for me to think about other things, such as tracking down that magna cum laude son-of-a-bitch and punching him square in the mouth.

Ben was sitting on his front step, beer in hand. He ran his fingers through his hair, pushing the loose strands away from his face. He stood up as I got closer, reaching his arms out and wrapping me up in him. I instantly felt my emotions threatening to surface. Endings always have a tendency sneak up on you, no matter how prepared you think you are.

He rubbed my back for a few moments more, eventually letting go and leading me into his apartment. His place was just as barren as mine. All that remained were several cardboard boxes and a six-pack sitting on the table. He opened a beer and handed it to me.

"This is weird."

I nodded in agreement. My attention shifted to the box marked, *For L.A.* I knelt down beside it, reaching in and pulling out the black frame sitting on top. It had collected a bit of dust over the last four years. But those eyes still looked the same. I cleaned the glass with my fingers.

"I love this picture of you."

I thought about freshman year. The nerves that had surged through my body right before I knocked on his door. His arm around me at that first party. I would do anything to go back to those early days. To do it all over again. There were so many things I would have done differently.

"Me too."

I was startled by his voice. *Had he heard me?*

"What did you say?"

He gave me a strange look. "I said, me too. I love that picture."

"Right..." I placed the frame back down and stood up.

"Well, I can't believe it's all over."

Ben's eyes moved around the empty room.

"Next week I'll be in Los Angeles and you'll be in New York."

"Does that mean we're adults?"

"I wouldn't go that far."

He finished off his beer, tossing the bottle into the trash. I walked over to the couch and threw myself down, leaning my head back against one of the cushions. Ben followed closely behind, settling into the chair across from me. He smiled at me and I smiled back.

"You're really moving to Los Angeles."

"Tom and I signed a lease for the first of June. Can you believe it?"

"No, I can't."

"More importantly, when am I going to see you again?"

I closed my eyes, still trying to push the reality of it all far from my mind. But my anxiety had other plans. It was now morphing into dread. I had been avoiding the change for so long that it now consumed me all at once. I became weak, sweaty. The walls felt like they were closing in on me. I could hear Ben talking, but his voice was distant and I couldn't make out what he was saying. I sat up, reaching my arm out in his direction.

"Perry?"

This is just like that dream. I'm running towards him. I reach out but he keeps slipping away. This is just like that dream. I'll never reach him.

"Perry? What are you doing?"

"I'll be right back."

What the fuck am I doing? I stood up without warning and dashed to the bathroom, unsure if I would even make it there before passing out. The second I closed the door I sank to the ground. I held my legs close to my chest, burying my head between them. Tears began to descend down my cheeks. *What is happening? Am I dying? Is this where it ends?*

"Perry? Are you alright?"

The knock on the door was urgent. I cleared my throat and blurted out the first thing that came to mind.

"I must have eaten something weird. It's going right through me." *Great. Now Ben thinks I'm taking a giant dump in his apartment.*

"Um...okay."

I rested my head against the outdated tile wall and sobbed quietly. Several minutes went by before he knocked again. This time the knock was soft, more unsure than anything else. I had no choice but to confront the situation head on. I took a deep breath, reaching my arm out and pushing on the door. It creaked open, revealing a concerned Ben squatting down on the other side.

"Alright, tell the truth. You weren't pooping."

He moved his hand towards my face, using his thumb to gently brush away a tear.

"I don't know what I'm doing, Ben. What are any of us doing?"

He sat down next to me. "Do you really want an answer to that, or is it more of a philosophical question?"

"I don't know. I don't know what I want." I lifted my head off the wall and turned towards him. "I think

I just had a panic attack. Or a heart attack. Or maybe both."

"You'll be fine, I promise. Today was a lot to take in, that's all."

"It's more than that Ben." I looked up at the ceiling. I couldn't stop the tears if I tried. "I'm really sad. I feel really sad."

My voice cracked as I said it. It was the most vulnerable I had ever been with him. He pulled me in close. My head rested on his shoulder. He stroked my hair as the tears continued to fall. And after a few minutes of silence, he spoke.

"Do you remember the night we first met?"

I nodded that I did. He continued to stroke my hair.

"I knelt down next to you and waited for you to open your eyes. And when you finally did, I thought there was something about you I had never known before. I knew it instantly, just by looking in your eyes. It was like nothing I had ever felt. I didn't know what to do. And then you opened your mouth and you had blood everywhere, I mean it was a fucking crime scene."

We both laughed. It was easy to picture that night. It felt like no time had passed.

"I remember thinking to myself that if I ever had the chance to tell you, I would tell you that you were the most beautiful girl I had ever laid eyes on. And then I got to know you and I thought that was so ridiculous. Telling you you're beautiful when there's so much more to it."

There were so many things I wanted to say to him. *I love you, Ben. I've been in love with you since the day I met you. I'm a fool. I'm complicated. I'm an emotional wreck. I've made mistakes. You've made mistakes. I haven't been able to open up to you because the fear of losing you is far greater than I can take.* But what would that do? What would saying any of that do? I'd open up to him and say out loud that I care about him more than I care about myself. Then in a few days he'd be on a plane to Los Angeles and I'd be in New York, and it wouldn't matter anymore. None of this mattered anymore.

"You had so much time to tell me this, Ben. You could have said *anything* over the last four years and you didn't. What am I supposed to do with this information now?"

I searched his face for answers.

"What do you want me to say, Perry? I fucked up. I didn't know what to do. I felt differently about you, but it was a lot to deal with. It's not like you did anything to help the situation."

"I need to go."

I stood up from the floor, pushing my way out of the bathroom. Ben scrambled after me.

"Perry, wait."

He grabbed for my arm. "Don't go, please."

"I have to go, Ben." I turned back to look at him one last time. His eyes were pleading. My tears intensified. I could barely get the words out. "Please let go. I have to go."

He reluctantly let go and I rushed towards the front door, shutting it behind me without another word. The sun had set and only darkness remained. I cried the entire walk home. The pain settling in my upper chest was unrelenting. Ben had just confessed what I had waited four years to hear. And then I walked out on him.

By the time I got home my eyes were bloodshot. I unlocked the door to find Ali sitting on the floor reading a magazine, a glass of wine at her feet. She stood up in an instant. Her carefree expression quickly vanished.

"Oh my god. What happened?"

She ran over to me, pulling me in close to her.

"Ben loves me."

She rubbed my back, ignoring the growing wet spot on her shoulder.

"Oh, Perry. I know. It's okay. I know. It's going to be alright."

That night, Ali and I lay in her bed and I listened as she tried to take my mind off of things. I had no words and that was all right. She played with my hair and reminisced. *We laughed. We cried. We fought. Remember the time I threw an entire container of french fries at you after winter formal? And who could forget Neil?*

I sighed, thinking life was so simple at Neil's. *The night before I met Ben.*

Have a little faith in humanity

Tuesday, May 29, 2007, 6:54am

My parents dropped me off at the bus station bright and early Tuesday morning. My dad reminded me at least three times on the car ride over, and once at the station, that they would be outside of my apartment on Friday at noon, *sharp*. I was to act like a responsible adult and meet them promptly, so we could unload the truck as quickly as possible.

"What would possibly prevent me from being there?"

My dad reached out and rested one hand on my shoulder. His tone was serious.

"Just remember what we talked about, Perry. Actions have consequences in the real world."

"Thank you for letting me know."

He grabbed the car keys from out of his pocket.

"Are you sure you don't want to wait and drive down with us on Friday?"

"I'm sure, Dad. I need to get this show on the road."

He leaned in and kissed me on the cheek. I waved them out of the parking lot and turned towards the bus with a new sense of purpose. *This is it. The first day of the rest of my life. Real world here I come.* I approached the bus driver and smiled, handing him my duffel bag to be placed in storage with the others.

"Thank you." I leaned in close to read the name on his tag. "Ronald. Thank you, Ronald."

His teeth were exceptionally unbrushed. Gray chest hairs poked out from between the loose buttons on his old company shirt. He ripped the bag from my hand and launched it carelessly into the storage compartment without giving it another thought. I glanced over his shoulder with concern for the well-being of my belongings. Not that there was much to be concerned about. It was basically a pile of sweatpants.

"Can I help you, sweetheart?"

His raspy voice was almost as terrifying as the blood oozing out of the scab on his hand.

"Yes, sorry. It's just...my bag is kind of fragile. You're bleeding. Did you know you're bleeding?"

"Next!"

The bus was still rather empty by the time I boarded and settled on a window seat near the front. I checked my phone. 6:56am. Only four minutes left to stress over some smelly jerk asking to sit next to me. I threw my purse down on the vacant aisle seat, making it extra clear that no one was to sit there.

I checked my phone again at 6:59am and became alarmed at the number of people still making their way towards the bus. *Don't these incompetent stragglers have clocks? We are leaving at 7am sharp, people.* I stared intently down at the screen, willing the last minute to tick by as quickly as possible. When it finally struck seven o'clock, I pressed my face up against the glass. *What the fuck is Ronald doing?* Ronald didn't seem to care much about being on time. In fact, he didn't seem to care much about anything other than taking a cigarette break before we even hit the road.

I turned my attention back to the front of the bus and that's when everything really started to unravel. That's when I laid eyes on *him* for the first time. He had just climbed to the top of the steps. He was panting wildly, using his arm to wipe the sweat from his brow. His belly was big. The biggest I had ever seen up close. He had unruly hair and a crusty brown stain all down the front of his cream-colored shirt. A shirt that had probably been a crisp white when he bought it the year I was born.

And then it happened. I accidentally made eye contact with him. *No. No. No. NO. WHY DID YOU DO THAT!? Why did you look up there?* He smiled at me and I immediately slumped over in an attempt to fake my own death. I closed my eyes tight, willing him to forget about the eye contact and find a seat at the very, very, very back of the bus. I could hear him wheezing his way down the aisle and then all at once the wheezing stopped. I was in the clear. I opened one eye just to make sure. He was standing directly over me.

"Excuse me, miss?"

I let out a few soft snores in one last desperate attempt to save the seat. *Keep walking. Keep walking. For the love of all things holy keep fucking walking.*

"Miss?"

Oh god, he's poking me. He's touching me. I slowly opened my eyes and yawned, stretching my arms out over my head. I looked up at him sheepishly.

"What?" I looked at my watch. "Are we in New York?"

He let out a chuckle that came from the depths of his round belly. He smelled of body odor and sharp cheese.

"We haven't even left New Hampshire yet. Is anyone sitting in this seat?"

"Um..." I turned around and saw that the aisle seat directly behind mine was empty. "This seat right here?"

The girl sitting behind me was around my age. She gave me an outraged look that had *eat a dick* written all over it. I didn't care. It was every man for themselves on the bus. Everyone knew that.

"No, miss. This seat right here next to you."

"Oh, this seat..." *Think Perry. Think. Fucking think. Help. Help. Help. Help. Help. Fuck me.* I sighed in defeat, moving my purse to my lap. "Yeah, it's free."

The trip to New York was all of five hours. For a majority of the ride I stared out the window, soulfully listening to Coldplay and applying every lyric to my current life status. I determined that "Green Eyes" was written about Ben and I. Except for the green eyes part. Mine were blue. The more I thought about it, the more every song seemed to be about Ben and me. *My life is tragic.*

For one hour in Massachusetts my seatmate's chair vibrated non-stop on account of the farts. I didn't really care. Maybe because they weren't smelly and I expected as much. I only truly lost my shit once around ten-thirty in the morning when a woman began to indulge in a sushi brunch.

"Why would you ever bring sushi on a bus? Seriously. So fucking disrespectful." I yelled it out passive-aggressively hoping someone, anyone, would agree with me. No one acknowledged the outburst. I hunched down in my seat, arms crossed over my chest. "This isn't the fucking Dollar Express, people. I paid thirty dollars for this ticket."

Traffic heading into the city was surprisingly tame and the bus hurdled its way to Port Authority without further incident. I descended the stairs and waited patiently for Ronald to place my duffel bag on the curb, this time with a little more dignity. When he finally fished it out from the back of storage, he stared at it long and hard. I smiled and extended my arms. Before I could grab ahold of the handle, Ronald let the duffel slip from between his fingers. It landed at his feet. His old boot kicked it over in my direction.

"Slippery little thing."

I snatched up the bag and held it close to my chest, turning to storm off. Almost instantly, I smashed into a woman with blonde teased hair, poorly painted eyebrows, and an all denim outfit, waiting to board her bus to Philadelphia. The impact sent me toppling backwards. As I lay on the ground of the Port Authority, I wondered if I should just get back on the bus and head right back to where I came from. *Maybe this was all a big mistake.* Then his face hovered over me. His wide smile temporarily restored my faith in humanity. He reached his hand down and pulled me to my feet.

"Took a bit of a tumble there. Better be careful next time. I'm Bill. It was nice to sit next to you."

"It was nice to sit next to you, Bill."

Appreciate honest friends

What, are you guys best friends now? You know he's gone down on me, right? This was Ali's reaction when she found out Ted and I had been exchanging text messages in the months following their breakup. On the one hand, I was happy to hear her openly saying such things as, *gone down on me*. She had come a long way since the day we met. On the other hand, it was an extreme overreaction. *I have class with him. He's funny. Calm down. Nobody wants to screw Ted.*

As it turned out, Ted quickly filled a void I didn't know existed. He became a trusted confidant. We understood each other. But more importantly, he was always honest even when it was really fucking hard to be honest. Ted and I had a genuine care for one another that wasn't muddled by sex or any other bullshit ulterior motive. I considered him more of a brother than anything else. So what if he liked to snort lines of whipped cream off of butt cracks? That was all hearsay anyways.

I had texted Ted the Sunday after graduation in a fit of desperation. Being home with my parents wasn't doing much to help my fragile emotional state. I needed the distraction of the city. My apartment wasn't available until Friday. He agreed that I could stay on his couch under one condition. I was not to act as a cockblock. I promised to keep my mouth shut about anything that went down. He then elaborated that not being a cockblock included leaving the apartment in the middle of the night if things were getting particularly steamy. I told him he was high maintenance, but agreed to it. Not that I had much of a choice.

I now stepped out of the Port Authority and onto the sidewalk. The humid Midtown air had a slight garbage stench. I didn't care. I had made it to the greatest city in the world. I closed my eyes and took a deep sniff of that garbage, already feeling a strange sense of authority over the people passing me on the street. These people were tired, beaten down zombies. I was young, fresh, and alive. I held my arm out with more confidence than ever. *Time to take control of my destiny.* To my surprise, a bright yellow cab pulled over immediately. *Fuck these peasants, I'm out.*

"Excuse me, miss."

"Hmm?"

Directly behind me stood a man wearing a reflective vest. He was manning the cab station.

"There's a line."

I glanced over his shoulder to see about twenty unamused travelers standing around with their luggage.

"Right. Sorry about that."

Thirty minutes later I slid out of a cab and into the front lobby of Ted's Gramercy Park apartment building. Ted would be at work until later tonight. He informed me that he had left a spare set of keys with his doorman. *Doorman.* Here I was, sweaty, dead broke, taking the crappy sushi bus with Ronald and his band of misfits, while Ted had a fucking doorman who dutifully stood watch during his wild sex parties.

"Wow…"

The foyer was magnificent with its mosaic tile flooring and oversized chandelier. I gazed up in awe. I had never seen anything like it.

"Can I help you?"

He kept a stern eye on my duffel bag. I backpedaled towards the desk, my attention still on the ceiling.

"That chandelier is amazing."

"Fine. What can I help you with?"

"Is it made out of gold?"

"No."

I pushed my unwashed hair away from my face and straightened out my shirt in an attempt to be taken more seriously. My forearm rested on the front desk. He narrowed his eyes, making it clear no forearms should be resting on the front desk.

"Yes. Hi. I'm staying with Ted Baker. He said he left some keys for me."

He studied a sheet of paper. "Ms. Walsh, is it?"

"Only on formal occasions."

"Excuse me?"

"I'm just kidding." I laughed. His face remained blank. I cleared my throat and continued. "I'm Ms. Walsh all the time, obviously."

"Right. Obviously."

He was unamused, bending down to grab a set of keys from beneath the desk.

"Mr. Baker resides in 4B. Take the elevator up to the fourth floor. When you get off the elevator, take a right. You will find 4B at the end of the hallway on the left. Mr. Baker is expected home around eight o'clock this evening."

"Great, thank you."

I sulked my way over to the elevator. For some strange reason I wanted him to like me. I wanted him to at least laugh at my jokes. I looked back in his direction, hoping to make eye contact one last time. He appeared to be actively avoiding my advances, shuffling papers that did not need shuffling.

"You know, I never did catch your name."

"I told it to you."

I raised an eyebrow and turned back to the elevator. The doors opened and I stepped in, pressing the button for the fourth floor. The whole ride up I tried desperately to recall his name. *Gerald. Mike. Harold. Max. Leslie. Leslie? That's what it was. Leslie. The femininity of it threw me off.*

Ted's apartment was everything I imagined it would be. It was a museum of fine artifacts and framed photographs of what looked to be generations of Baker men. I picked one up. In it, a dapper looking man wearing a tuxedo leaned up against a bar. He had a thick head of slicked, black hair. He was the sexiest person from the olden days I had ever seen. His stare was piercing. He was looking right at me, giving me the eyes. *I will be masturbating to you before the week is up.*

I made my way over to the living room and threw myself down on the couch, resting my hands on my chest and closing my eyes. The next thing I knew I heard a voice. At first the voice was distant, somewhat muffled. *Perry. Perry. Perry.* I pictured the sexy man from the photograph. His ghost was drifting towards me, brought back from the dead to make love to me. Making love to me was the only way he could finally ascend to the land of eternal happiness. As the ghost floated closer his voice got deeper, more urgent. *Perry. Perry. Perry.*

"Let's do it, ghost."

"What? Wake up."

I opened my eyes to find Ted slapping my arm.

"Oh my god, what?" I shot up from the couch. "What time is it?"

He looked over at the clock. "A little after seven. Do you know what you just said?"

I yawned and rubbed my eyes. "Yeah, yeah something about a ghost. By the way, who is that man in the photograph over there?"

I pointed at the glass table. Ted's gaze followed my finger. "That's my grandfather."

"Is he still alive?"

"No. He died five years ago."

"Sorry for your loss."

A horrified expression washed over his face. *He's onto us.* He reached behind me and yanked a couch pillow out from underneath my ass, pointing aggressively at the wet spot in the corner.

"You drooled all over my pillow."

I shrugged. "Okay."

He made an exaggerated circular motion around the spot. "Drool. All over."

"Don't be dramatic."

"This pillow cost me over three hundred dollars, Perry."

I stood up and walked over to the kitchen to get some water.

"Why the hell would anyone buy a pillow for three hundred dollars?"

I searched the cabinets for a glass, reaching for one and turning on the sink. Ted dropped the pillow in an instant and rushed over to my side. He snatched the glass from my hand and dumped the water out.

"Don't drink that. I have filtered water in the fridge."

He opened the refrigerator and poured me a glass of his *special water*. I was positive there was no difference, but who was I to argue with Mr. Baker. Besides, I had bigger issues right now, like how to get myself a copy of that framed picture.

"Anyways. Surprise. I'm home early. I figured you'd want to do something special on your first night as a New Yorker."

"Hanging out with you is not special."

I chugged the entire glass of the water. Only now did it occur to me that I hadn't had anything to eat or drink all day. I walked over to the fridge and filled the glass a second time.

"Go take a shower and we'll get out of here."

"I just showered yesterday."

He looked up from sorting the mail. "Well shower again. It's your first fucking night in New York. Be better. Be the new and improved Perry."

I decided that becoming the new and improved Perry meant using Ted's razor to shave my legs, armpits, and pubic area in that order. Within one hour I was dressed. The two of us stood waiting for the elevator. I hummed to myself as Ted side-eyed me.

"Did you use my razor?"

"No."

"We'll see about that."

The elevator dinged and the doors opened slowly. I stepped in and stood next to a woman wearing an oversized pair of black sunglasses. It seemed forced, like she was making a great effort to remain anonymous. This clearly was not working because I recognized her almost instantly, though I couldn't quite place her. Ted gave her a discreet nod. Her face remained unchanged.

The three of us rode in complete silence. When we reached the ground level she spilled out into the lobby, quickly exiting the building and jumping into waiting town car. Leslie practically tripped over himself trying to escort her out. His friendly act came to an abrupt halt once he found himself face-to-face with me. He quickly diverted his attention to Ted.

"Have a wonderful evening, Mr. Baker."

"Thank you, AJ, same to you."

AJ? Ted held the door open for me. Once outside, I linked my arm through his as we walked down 20th Street and made our way towards Third Avenue. The humidity had let up a bit and it was turning out to be a beautiful night.

"Your doorman told me his name was Leslie."

"Perry, no. He would never do that."

"Yes, he did. Why would I just make that up?"

"You make things up all the time, Perry. You create these stories in your head and then try to play them off as truths."

"He treats me like I'm a homeless drifter."

"You are a homeless drifter."

"Meanwhile, some lady with big sunglasses struts through the lobby and he pisses all over himself."

"That was Lisa Shawn."

I stopped dead in my tracks right in the middle of Third Avenue, grabbing at my heart.

"Oh my god, Ted. I'm hyperventilating."

"You're perfectly fine. Come on, keep walking."

"That was my first celebrity encounter, *ever*. Did you happen to know an actress was living in your building?"

Ted was becoming impatient. He stood on the sidewalk, motioning with both hands for me to keep moving forward. A cab driver held down his horn.

"Here's your first lesson for living in New York. Cabbies don't care about you. They don't give a shit about your life. Cabbies are crazy motherfuckers. They will run you down and go to bed feeling content."

"Answer my question."

"We slept together. Are you happy? Now move it!"

Relax on the bread basket

Tuesday, May 29, 2007, 8:44pm

Ted agonized over the wine list for an unreasonable amount of time. I couldn't take my eyes off of him. I was searching for any visible sign that what he said on the street was a lie. *There's no way he had sex with Lisa Shawn. Did he have sex with Lisa Shawn?* I had to admit, he did look rather appealing in his crisp, white button-down, topped off with a fresh spray tan.

"What would be your personal recommendation, Claire?"

I rolled my eyes and dug into the bread basket. Claire leaned forward against the side of his body. Her right breast brushed up against his shoulder. Her left breast was practically in his mouth. Ted glanced up from the wine list and winked at me. I couldn't take it anymore.

"Just surprise us."

My mouth was full when I blurted it out. Claire jumped at the sound of my voice. It was as if she had completely forgotten that I was sitting right across the table. Ted glared at me for ruining his fun, snapping the wine list shut.

"The lady wants to be surprised."

"No problem. I'll be right back."

"Thanks, Claire."

Their hands overlapped in the exchanging of the wine list. Claire blushed, turning quickly to find the perfect bottle for her new love interest. I leaned forward against the table.

"Do you have a small penis? Is that why you act this way?"

"You wish you knew what my penis looked like."

I picked up another piece of bread, spreading an entire butter ball over the top of the roll.

"That is so gross, Perry. Cut the roll open before you butter it."

"You don't have to cut the roll open when you eat it like this."

I shoved the entire thing into my mouth, pushing the last of it in with my fingertips just as Claire returned with her selection. She held the bottle out towards Ted, discussing the mixture of grapes. A small piece of roll broke free and trickled down my throat, sending me into a panic. My eyes began to water. I reached for my napkin, covering my mouth as I coughed and gagged.

"Oh my god! Are you choking?"

Claire rushed over to my side. Ted rolled his eyes. It was night one and I was already acting as a cockblock.

"She's fine. Anyways, what were you saying about the grapes?"

I spit the entire roll out into my napkin, making exaggerated throw up sounds. Ted covered his mouth with his hand and looked away. After examining the partially-chewed roll for blood, I folded the napkin carefully and placed it down on the table. I took a sip of water, clearing my throat twice to make sure it was all out. Claire stood next to me, eyes wide. I looked up at her and smiled.

"I'm fine, thanks. What were you saying about full-bodied?"

"Um..."

She stared down at the napkin, a horrified expression on her face. Ted attempted to divert the attention back to him by taking a taste of the wine and declaring it exquisite. Claire laughed nervously and quickly filled our glasses, placing the bottle down in the center of the table. She took a deep breath and reached for the napkin.

"I'll be right back to take your order..."

She ran off to the kitchen, where I'm sure she puked all over herself. I picked up the bottle of wine and filled my glass to a more appropriate level.

"Let's just be honest with ourselves about the size of a pour."

Ted leaned forward, angrily whispering at me. "Let's just be honest with ourselves about the fact that that was the most appalling thing I have ever seen."

I shrugged. "I choked."

"You shoved an entire roll into your mouth."

"Get over yourself. She probably has a boyfriend."

"Alright then. Let's forget about that. Let's talk about why you're here."

"On this planet or in this restaurant?"

"Why you are here. In New York City. On a Tuesday. Sleeping on my couch."

I sat back in my chair and scoffed. How dare he. He didn't know what I had been through.

"For your information, *Ted*, there was a very tragic ending to my college career and I don't know if I'm ready to talk about it."

"Don't be defensive, Perry. I just want to help."

"I'm sure."

If I was going down this road with him, I needed to be less sober. I chugged the rest of my wine, refilling the glass as I thought about what it was that I wanted to say.

"Where should I start? Let's see. Hmmm...oh, right." My eyes narrowed in on him and it all came spewing out. "I feel confused. I feel emotionally wrecked. I feel regretful. I feel sad. I feel like a terrible person. I feel angry. I sleep with people who are nuts. I feel incapable of being loved by someone. I feel like I'm hanging on by a fucking thread."

I leaned back, folding my arms over my chest. My bottom lip started to quiver. I closed my eyes to reign it in. *You are not going to cry.* He sat swirling his wine around in the glass, taking time to process what I had just said. His demeanor had completely changed and I could tell by his body language that he felt badly for poking at me. He took a sip of his wine and placed his glass back down on the table, opening his mouth to speak.

"First of all, you are not incapable of being loved. I love you, you know that." He took another sip of wine. "Second of all, if this is about Ben, which I'm sure it is, you know where I stand on this. He is an asshole who strung you along for years. You are way too good for him, Perry."

"He's not an asshole. It's just...I can't explain it. It's complicated."

"Alright, say I'm wrong, which I never am by the way. But say I'm wrong this one time and he's not an asshole. Let's simply look at the facts."

"You don't know all of the facts."

"I do know that this guy is a genius because he ran around with a girlfriend for years, while somehow still managing to sleep with you whenever he wanted."

"I did some fucked up things too. I'm not exactly a saint."

Ted sat back and shook his head. "My god, Perry. Come on. This isn't your fault."

"I'm just saying, there's more to the Perry and Ben story than you will ever know, or understand. Than anyone will."

"Do you know what my favorite part of the Perry and Ben story is?"

"Please, enlighten me."

"My favorite part was when you slept with him and then he broke up with Alex for the second time. You were all excited thinking it was your big chance. The both of you were finally going to grow the hell up and ride off into the sunset together. You were *this* close to having little Ben and Perry babies running around, but then, what was it? What did he do? Take it away, Perry."

"You're an asshole."

"That's right. He slept with Brooke." His eyes were wide. He leaned forward, resting his elbows on the table. "Who he then stayed with for a year. During which time, you were still sleeping with him, of course. Are you not seeing the pattern here?"

"He didn't love her."

"Oh, right." He relaxed in his chair. "I forgot. He loves you."

Do not drink and text

Wednesday, May 30, 2007, 9:56am

I shot up from the couch drenched in sweat. For a second I had no idea where I was. My head was pounding. I lay back down, kicking the throw blanket to the floor. My armpits oozed the worst kind of body odor.

"Ted..." I rolled over to face the back of the couch. "Ted, I think I'm dying. I need water ASAP. Filtered water."

My demands were met with silence.

"Ted, seriously. I'm gonna throw up all over this three hundred dollar pillow."

More silence.

I glanced over at the clock. *9:56am.* It suddenly occurred to me that it was a Wednesday. Ted had most likely been at work for a solid two hours already. I reached down for my phone, yawning as I flipped it open. *Holy shit.* My blood froze. I slammed the phone shut, pressing it against my chest. My mind raced. I struggled to remember the details of last night. I closed my eyes hoping it would help. Little snippets of conversation began to trickle back. *Real men smoke a pack a day and don't wear sunscreen. Beer and wine mixed together tastes like candy! Don't text him. You'll hate yourself in the morning. Chlamydia is curable, but it still totally sucks.*

Beer and wine does not taste like candy and DON'T TEXT HIM. YOU'LL HATE YOURSELF IN THE MORNING. I tried my best to remain calm. This was probably just like that time junior year when I got worked up about drunk texting Bobby from next door after game night. I blew it so out of proportion that I had convinced myself I had texted him, *I'm going to murder a BUNCH of puppies.* After a full day of avoiding my phone, I finally opened it to see that I had written, *Fun time tonight!* To which he responded, *Indeed!* A completely harmless exchange.

This was probably just like that time. *Probably.* I paced around Ted's fluffy, white living room rug, staring anxiously at the coffee table. The fact of the matter was, there were very real text messages in that phone that needed to be read, and I needed to woman up and read them. I took a deep breath, snatching the phone from the table. *Be the new and improved Perry.*

12:36am

Me: Hi

Ben: Hi

Twenty minute delay.

Ben: So how bout them Yankees...

Me: I miss you

Ben: I miss you too...how's life in the real world?

Me: With Ted at dive bar

Ben: I don't trust that guy

Me: I wish I could see you

Ben: I know what you mean...

I slammed the phone shut. *I know what you mean, dot dot dot.* What kind of cruel mind game was this? What was he trying to say with those dots? Those dots could mean anything. My body was becoming physically and mentally overcome by events. Sweat continued to drench my underwear. A wet trickle rolled down my spine and squeezed its way between my butt cheeks. *I'm going to be sick.*

I needed to get to the bathroom and I needed to get there fast. I had taken one step towards the hallway when my body gave in. Projectile vomit pushed its way up my esophagus, spewing out of my mouth and all over the rug. *Beer and wine. It's totally not okay. It's never okay.*

Do not sneak up on someone

Friday, June 1, 2007, 6:30am

It had been a week that had proven more emotionally consuming than any that had come before. I felt unhinged, like my sanity was hanging in the balance. A feeling that was only exacerbated by the fact that I was living on someone else's couch. I was a drifter, a misplaced member of society. I slept on a piece of furniture that Ted jerked off on constantly. Blowing his load while his ass sat right on the three hundred dollar pillow I cuddled up to every night. *Right where you lay your head,* he told me. *Sweet dreams.*

Rifling around in my duffel bag, I found there wasn't much left in terms of wardrobe options. I was at the end of my stay with Ted and the sweatsuit I had skulked around in for a majority of the week had taken up most of the space.

I opted for some black yoga pants and an old spray-painted Spice Girls shirt. Years ago, I had insisted that my dad purchase the shirt for me on a

New Jersey boardwalk. *I need it!* I screamed it at him in front of hundreds of strangers. He smiled and promptly purchased it. Once we were back within the safe confines of the car he told me to take a good, hard look. I wouldn't see that shirt again until Christmas, *if* I was lucky.

My sneakers hit the pavement and I headed west on 20th Street towards the small bagel shop I had frequented every morning since my arrival. My order was always the same, one small black coffee and one bagel with extra cream cheese. This morning I ordered two small black coffees. I was feeling generous, and Ted should consider it generous given the fact that I had thirty-six dollars left in my checking account.

Knowing Ted, I would get back to the apartment and he would promptly inform me that he only drank large coffees. I would be forced to confess that even if I had all the money in the world, I still wouldn't buy him a large coffee. He would then tell me it was a good idea to save my money to pay for the professional cleaning of his rug, the one that still had traces of my green vomit crusted into it. I wouldn't pay for the rug because it was hideous. By the time I pulled the key from the lock and swung the apartment door open, our whole morning had already played out in my mind. The clock on the microwave read 7:23am. I kicked the door shut with my leg and placed both coffees down on the kitchen counter.

"Ted?"

He had to be awake by now. It was a work day. I walked down the hallway towards his bedroom. His door was still shut. I knocked softly and stood with my ear pressed firmly against it.

"Ted?"

I turned the knob and opened the door a crack. I could hear water running from the shower. Without another word, I carefully shut the door and scampered back down the hallway to look for anything I could use to scare the shit out of him. I picked up a navy-blue umbrella from a wicker basket. *What would a burglar do with an umbrella? Probably stab someone, that's what. Beat someone over the head with it. Too aggressive.* I opened the closet door and eyed a black winter scarf hanging from one of the hooks. I yanked it down and wrapped it around my face several times, leaving only a small slit for my eyes.

I tiptoed back towards the bedroom, my hot morning breath quickly collected in the woolen material. *It's so itchy.* Ever so slowly, I twisted the doorknob, peeking my head around the corner like a bandit. The bathroom door was open just a hair. An alternative rock station was blaring from the shower radio. I dropped down on the floor and began to slither my way towards the opening. Steam billowed out into the bedroom. An emo voice crooned about love being a radioactive tentacle, whatever the fuck that meant. I took a deep breath. It was time. All at once I shot up from the ground, karate kicking the door so hard that it flung open and smashed against the wall behind it.

"Give me all your money small – OH MY GOD!"

"What the fuck?!"

Through the glass I saw not one, but two bodies. A curvy brunette was bent over in front. Ted stood behind her, both of their hands were plastered up against the glass, alongside of her nipples. She looked up in sheer horror, letting out an elongated scream. I covered my eyes with both hands, peeking between my fingers only once to make sure it was real.

"Oh my god, *Ted*! When did she get here?"

The girl moved quickly, shielding her naked body with his.

"Is this your wife?!"

Ted covered his dick with his hands "No, this isn't my fucking wife. Get the fuck out, Perry!"

"I can't move! I can't feel my legs! Help me!"

The shock of it all had left my body frozen in place. My feet felt as though they weighed a hundred pounds each. I couldn't pick them up off the floor if I tried. Ted rolled his eyes and made exaggerated arm motions towards my legs, leaving his uncovered dick in plain sight.

"You're fine. Let's go, chop chop. Get the fuck out of here, Perry! I mean it. Take my fucking scarf off of your face and get out."

He turned back around to see that the girl was now in hysterics.

"Why are you crying?"

"I can see your balls! Cover them up!"

"No, I will not cover them up! This is my bathroom!"

By the grace of God, I regained feeling in my lower body and rushed out of there as fast as I could. I sprinted into the living room, haphazardly shoving my belongings into my duffel bag. I was almost clear out the door when I realized I didn't have my coffee. I wasn't leaving without it. It was a decent percentage of my net worth. I ran back towards the kitchen, passing a mirror on the way and yelling out when I caught a glimpse of myself with the scarf still wrapped around my face.

"You're an idiot. This was a terrible idea."

I ripped it from my head and tossed it carelessly behind me. I grabbed the coffee and considered taking the picture of Ted's grandfather, before ultimately deciding against it. He would have to live in my memory now. The door shut behind me and I was safe, but not out of the woods. I ran up to the elevator, punching the down button several times like an asshole, hoping it would speed up the process. I paced back and forth, watching the floor numbers drop. *Eight, seven, six. Do not stop at six! Fuck you six!* Thirty second delay. *Five, four.*

When the doors opened I practically threw myself in, tripping and falling to the ground. I lay still next to my duffel bag for a several seconds, the elevator doors closing at my feet. *Ted's dick. Glass nipples.*

"Good lord, are you alright?"

"What?"

I rolled onto my back. My eyes widened. I scrambled to get up as quickly as possible, dusting off my yoga pants. The facial fillers made her expression hard to read. If I had to guess, I'd say she seemed mostly surprised with a hint of disgust. I tried to play it cool, leaning casually to the side.

"I'm good. I'm great actually. And you, Lisa Shawn?"

Her eyes stayed planted on me. A nervous smile crept across my face. I'm sure I looked utterly terrifying. *What was I doing? I couldn't lie to Lisa Shawn.* I suddenly felt compelled to tell her everything. Ted. The curvaceous brunette. The stuff between Ben and me. The time I slept with Darth Vader. All of it.

"So, actually it's a funny story." I paused, glancing over to see if she was still interested in how I was doing. This time her facial expression seemed to read, fucking *get on with it already.*

"Right, so anyways. To be honest with you Lisa Shawn."

"You don't need to say my full name like that."

"Right. Sorry. To be honest with you Lisa, I just walked in on my friend having sex with a complete stranger in the shower. Well, she was a stranger to me. I'm not sure if she was a stranger to him. I'm not even sure how she got into the apartment. I sleep on the couch, which is very close to the front door. They were doing it doggy style. It was a lot to take in. I'm just not feeling like myself these days, so it's hard. But I'm trying to move past it."

I cleared my throat and looked away. That was a lot of information. Lisa pursed her lips together. She was contemplating something. She eyed me up and down. I pretended to brush my yoga pants off a bit more, thinking she must be repulsed by the dirt and miscellaneous elevator pubes that were plastered all over me.

"Are those the Spice Girls?"

I looked down at my shirt. "Yes."

She turned her entire body to face me.

"Well, I hope for your sake you didn't come all the way to New York from whatever bumpkin town you're from with some romantic notion that a love affair would develop between the two of you. In the year that Ted Baker has lived in this building, his apartment has seen more pussy than a gynecologist."

"No. It's not like that. We really are just friends. I saw his dick for the first time, so I'm a little rattled. I'm making a mountain out of a small hill."

She laughed, appearing somewhat sympathetic to my condition.

"Mole hill. And I hope that wasn't the first time you've seen a dick."

"Oh, no." I scoffed at this suggestion. "God no, I've seen plenty of dicks. But not that many dicks. The right amount of dicks someone should see by my age. Maybe a handful. A handful of dicks." I looked up to the ceiling for answers. "Plus one."

"So, you've seen six dicks."

"Roughly."

"Did you count Ted's?"

"Seven. Seven dicks."

Let the past be the past

"Hey, it's me."

A siren wailed in the background. Voices became clear, faded out, and then became clear again. I closed my eyes and pictured Ben walking down the street. His stride purposeful, black sunglasses covering his big brown eyes. It was sunny of course, not a cloud in the sky. It's always sunny in Los Angeles, I imagined.

"Who is this?"

"You know who it is."

"What if I have an *it's me* kind of relationship with someone else by now?"

"Then I guess I'm in trouble."

I smiled, rolling over in bed to face the window overlooking 51st Street. I rested my head in my hand. A flash of lightning lit up the night sky, closely followed by the roar of thunder off in the distance. A couple walked hand-in-hand towards the entrance of a tavern across the street.

"So. Is New York everything you hoped it would be?"

"I guess. I haven't been out much, to tell you the truth. Our apartment is decent. Erin did a good job picking it out."

I pushed my window open a bit more. There was nothing better than listening to rain hit the pavement on a stormy summer night.

"And how is Erin? Tell her I've missed her terribly."

"I will. She's currently teetering on the edge of a breakdown ever since Kevin broke up with her."

"Kevin. Poor bastard."

"How's Los Angeles?"

My eyes were still following the couple from the street. The woman was beautiful, her long, dark hair was pulled back into a sleek ponytail. The man's sleeves were rolled up, the top buttons of his white shirt left open, exposing part of his chest. He whispered something in her ear. She let out a laugh that echoed down the street. Their hands parted. He reached for the door and held it open. He looked up at the sky, holding his hand out to touch the first fresh drops of rain. They disappeared into the tavern just as the skies opened up and it began to pour.

"Let's put it this way. For the first time in four years I can't hear Tom's sexual escapades through the wall. Our bedrooms are on opposite sides of the apartment."

"Now *that* is great news." I sat up, crossing my legs under me.

"You know how he operates. '*Oh, Jane...Jane...JANE...JAAANE!*' That was an accurate time lapse, in case you were wondering."

"What was that, ten seconds?"

"Generous."

I laughed. It was a genuine laugh that came from deep within. I realized I hadn't laughed like that in a long time. I thought about the girl from the street. The way she lifted her head and closed her eyes before her laughter filled the quiet night air. The way the man leaned in and whispered into her ear, kissing her neck before he moved away. They were happy. More than happy. They were exactly where they wanted to be. *Content.* I envied them. I didn't know the last time I felt content. I didn't know what I felt anymore.

"I think about you a lot, Perry."

"Oh yeah, what about me?"

A tear slid down my cheek. I quickly brushed it away. The last thing I wanted was for Ben to catch on to how emotional I still was. I wanted to shield him from my problems, but at the same time, I felt him slipping away from me. That fact alone was unbearable.

"Mostly the sex. But sometimes I think about your personality too."

"Aw, Ben." I rested my head back against the wall and closed my eyes. "That's the nicest thing anyone has ever said to me."

"Everything I said that night, I meant it. It's important that you know that."

"I know."

"I love you, Perry. I'm always here for you."

"Me too." The tears were flowing freely now. My bottom lip began to quiver, the telltale sign that things were only going downhill from here.

"Alright, Ben. I gotta go."

"You alright?"

"Yeah. Just tired." I brought my knees to my chest and buried my face in them. "We'll talk soon, okay?"

"Alright, Perry. I'll talk to you later."

"Bye, Ben."

I hung up the phone and sobbed under the covers for over an hour, until I was all dried up. There were no tears left. I stood in front of the bathroom mirror that night and made a vow to myself. I wouldn't cry over him ever again. He was Ben. My Ben. He would always be my Ben. There was nothing to cry about. Things were just going to be different now.

Somewhere along the way, Ben and I had morphed from two eighteen-year-old kids who met in a dorm to twenty-somethings who needed to get on with it. The faster I could accept that, the faster I could get on with my life. I didn't move to New York to wallow in what might have been. I moved to New York to take hold of what could be. *Be stronger than this. You're not sad anymore. You're content. You're the girl on the street. Be content like the girl on the street.*

Enjoy the grind

Monday, August 27, 2007, 5:01am

I lay there, wide awake, two hours before my alarm was set to go off. It was my first official day of work. Despite the fact that my career advisor predicted my future would be nothing short of an abysmal failure, a friend of a friend knew someone who worked in production at a well-known late night talk show. I would be starting as a production assistant, getting people coffee and figuring out how to fix a broken copy machine. But it was a job, and I could potentially rub elbows with the writers, maybe even some celebrities. Who knows, a celebrity might even take a liking to me, sweep me off my feet, and jet off with me. Until then, the pay was decent and there were benefits. If I played my cards right, I could survive on ramen noodles during the week while racking up impressive bar tabs on the weekends.

Manhattan was now in the throes of August. The city air was unbearably thick by the time the sun came up. While most people chose to evacuate, I stayed put. Not that I had much of a choice. I was dead broke. It was by choice, however, that I kept my bedroom windows open during some of the stickiest summer nights. The noise coming in off the street was a necessary distraction. Without it, I would be left in solitary confinement with my thoughts. I would lie motionless for hours, staring up at the ceiling, fixating on the fact that I had gone the entire summer without talking to *him*.

A month ago, I was feeling a little brave and a lot buzzed. I took a seat on the couch armed with a glass of wine and a laptop. Ben wasn't much for social media, more of an innocent bystander in other people's internet musings. But from what I could gather, he and Tom appeared to spend a lot of late nights hanging out with a trio of blonde-haired girls who liked leather jackets and went heavy on the dark lipstick. Someone named Shannon tagged him in several group photos. Nothing scandalous. Just your standard pics: arm-over-arm, smiling at the camera, bunny ears. And just when I thought I was in the clear, I spotted it.

The post was captioned *Future Lovers.* In it, Ben sat in a booth, his arm thrown around some girl named Dana. Dana was leaning her body into his, her hand touching his thigh as she whispered something in his ear. I zoomed in on the picture, analyzing if for thirty minutes. *What is she saying? Ben can't really be into her. She's got big boobs and fake eyelashes. That's so not Ben's type. I'm Ben's type. Is she rubbing his thigh or is her hand there for the picture? What the fuck is she saying? His smile doesn't look real. He's faking it. Are they in love? Did they have sex? Oh my god, they had sex. He had sex with Dana. They are together. They are a couple. I fucking hate Shannon. Why do you post these fucking lame pictures of your lame life?* I became so worked up at the thought of Ben being someone's future, or current, lover that I slammed the laptop shut and ate an entire jumbo bag of candy while cocooned in the comfort of a fleece blanket. *I hope he has a fucking perfect life with Dana and her secrets.*

That was the only major slip up I counted on the road to a more mature, peaceful adult existence. And it was all behind me now. I had a job. I had a yellow blouse and a white pair of pants laid out on a chair. I bought heels. Actual high heels that I would wear to work. Up to this point, I relied solely on flip flops and fuzzy boots to get me through every season. I had even rehearsed a routine in the week leading up to this day. *Stretch, shower, breakfast, blow-dry, makeup.* There was no longer idle time to sit around and ponder whether Ben's hands were on Dana's breasts last night. And they certainly were not on her breasts. Not a chance.

Within one hour I was out the door and headed to work, leaving Erin fast asleep in her bed. The studio was located a few blocks away on Broadway. It was no more than a five minute walk. I made sure to leave plenty of time to account for various emergency situations. *Sinkhole, tornado, sidewalk closure, coffee shop fire.* Within minutes, I was standing outside of the building, coffee in hand. Everything had gone seamlessly. I looked down at my watch. *Thirty minutes early.* I opened the door and walked up to the weary looking gentleman sitting behind the front desk. *Another zombie.* I extended my hand towards him. He yawned without covering his mouth.

"I'm Perry. It's my first day."

His limp, cold hand met mine.

"Lenny. Elevator on your right, fifth floor."

His eyes drifted back to the newspaper. I looked down the hallway at the elevator, then back at Lenny.

"Are you sure it's the fifth floor? The last time I was here I went to the second floor."

His voice stayed flat. "All new hires report to the fifth floor. Thank you. Have a great day."

"Okay...thanks."

I walked hesitantly towards the elevator, looking back at Lenny only once. He chuckled at something he read in the paper, crossing his arms above his protruding belly. Questions swirled in my mind. *Are there any normal people in real life? Is there only hopelessness? What is that newspaper? I'll have to get a copy.* Lenny was mindlessly grinding out his life and it wasn't the kind of grinding I was used to, or welcomed. I wanted to come to work and change the world, escape my personal life, not be subjected to Lenny's mediocre existence.

The fifth floor was a shit storm of chaos. People ran back and forth, going about their daily routine as if I wasn't standing right there. I felt like a ghost. No one even looked up to say hello or question what the hell I was doing there. I stepped up to the front desk and waited. Papers were scattered every which way. I picked one up. It appeared to be part of a script. *This looks important.* A phone rang from somewhere under the mess and I jumped back, throwing the paper down on the desk and moving away.

I walked over to the window and looked down at the bustle of Broadway. Despite the chaos unfolding around me, this was where I wanted to be. I was in the middle of everything. This was the exact reason I moved to New York City in the first place. I would have to call my dad later and break the news that not all actions have consequences. Sometimes your actions are outrageous and everything still seems to work out in your favor.

My eyes landed on a handsome, silver-haired man walking briskly down the street in a suit and tie. He was carrying a briefcase and talking on his cell phone. His aviators made him sexy in a mysterious way. *No wedding ring. He just got divorced. He's looking to be someone's daddy.*

"Are you here for someone?"

"No. What? Sorry."

I spun around to find a tall, dark-eyed girl with short black hair and severely cut bangs. Her style had an edge to it that I could never pull off. She stood confused, her head tilted to one side.

"Hi. No. I'm here for myself. I'm Perry."

She walked around to the back of her desk and sat down, carelessly wiping the script pages away from her keyboard and sending them fluttering towards the ground.

"Am I missing something?"

"Sorry, no. I'm Perry. I just got hired in production. This is my first day."

"Oh." She began typing furiously, eyes locked on the screen. "Are you nervous?"

I hadn't really thought about it. "I guess a little. I just graduated. This is my first real job."

She stopped typing and leaned back in her chair, crossing one leg over the other.

"Do you have a boyfriend?"

"No. No boyfriend."

"Good. You don't want to muddy the waters with a boyfriend. Keep things simple."

She started up again with the furious typing. She seemed a little odd and distractible, but there was something about her that I instantly connected to.

"I'm Perry."

She didn't even bother to look at me. "You already said that."

"Oh, right."

She motioned in the direction of the hallway. "You're looking for Michael. He's in the back. He's in the depths of a midlife crisis and is a sexual harassment lawsuit waiting to happen. He's also your boss." She looked up and grinned. "Go get 'em."

Do not touch the mugs in the coffee shop

Wednesday, October 10, 2007, 6:43am

It was a dreary morning. I woke to the sound of raindrops pattering against my window. The rhythmic beat of the weather made for the kind of mood that screamed, *lounge in bed all morning with a cup of tea and a pair of cozy socks.* I lingered in the moment for as long as I could, pulling the comforter up to my chin and closing my eyes. It didn't take long to find myself drifting off again, my body jolted back to reality by the sound of a car alarm shattering through the morning calm. I yawned, reluctantly pushing the comforter to the side and rolling out of bed.

It was just another Wednesday. A rainy, autumn Wednesday. I've found that's the way life usually works. One morning you wake up and everything is exactly as it has always been. You go about your business like it's any other day. Then without warning, everything changes. One instant sets off a chain reaction and suddenly you find yourself swept up in an entirely new direction. A direction you never even dreamed was possible. It happens so quickly that you barely have time to breathe, let alone think. And that's the beauty of it all.

On this particular rainy Wednesday, I entered the coffee shop at 8:03am instead of my usual 7:45am sharp. I joined the back of the line, anxiously willing the patrons in front of me to hurry the hell up. Not that Michael would even notice that I was running behind. I'm sure he wouldn't grace us with his presence for another hour or so.

"I'll have a non-fat, double-shaken, double-dipped, flipped-upside-down, large caramel espresso latte, mild heat, no caramel, two sugars, extra foam."

What the fuck? What the fuck?! Are you fucking kidding me, lady? Just get a goddamn fucking regular coffee, you fucking moron! Fucking hurry the hell up with your fucking shoulder pads.

"Great. Will that be all for you today?"

Yes.

"I'll also have a breakfast sandwich with sausage, no cheese."

Fuck you, you fucking asshole. I will fucking destroy you if that breakfast sandwich takes longer than thirty seconds to produce.

And then it happened. In the middle of my inner tirade against Shoulderpads and her sausage breakfast, he rushed in off the street holding a briefcase over his head. I turned at the sound of the doorbell. His eyes met mine instantly. They were a deep brown hue, in stark contrast to the rain-dampened dirty blonde hair he ran his fingers through.

An overwhelming sensation spread throughout my entire body. I needed to know him. I needed to be near him. I needed to hear him speak my name. I was so taken aback by the feeling that it became impossible to concentrate on anything else. I didn't even notice when Shoulderpads began incessantly rapping her stick-on fingernails against the counter as she waited for that goddamn sandwich.

He shook the raindrops from his briefcase. When he looked up, we locked eyes for a second time. I smiled at him. At least I think I was smiling. I couldn't feel my face. His eyes softened and he let out a quiet laugh. He held his hand up as he mouthed one simple word, *hello*. The sound of his laugh played over and over again in my mind until it clicked. I was staring. The entire time he had been in that coffee shop I had not taken my eyes off of him once. When the feeling returned to my face, I realized that my mouth was hanging open. I slowly closed it and turned my attention back to the front of the line. *I'm a psycho.*

But I couldn't ignore the sensation. Everything in my being ached for this stranger. It was a tingling that took hold of my insides and raged through my veins. Against my better judgement, I discreetly glanced over my right shoulder to find that his eyes were still planted on me. He raised one eyebrow in my direction. I pretended to admire a mug that was on sale for $5.99.

"Miss, what can I get you?"

"Um." I fumbled with the mug, using both hands to steady it on the shelf. *Where was I?* "Sorry. I'll just have a small coffee."

"Please don't touch the mugs."

"Sorry. I'm sorry."

"That's a display. If you actually want a mug, which I'm sure you don't, I'll get one from the supply closet."

"Um..."

I looked back to see that he was biting his lip. He was amused by all of this.

"Yes...I'll take the mug."

I left the coffee shop that morning knowing two things in this world were certain. Number one: a good-looking man, not a boy, but a man wearing an actual suit to his adult job had smiled at me. *Twice*. Number two: Even with the sale price, I overpaid for a shitty white mug that read, **IT'S COFFEE TIME SOMEWHERE,** in bold black font.

The rest of the day was completely shot. I sat at my desk, resting my head in my hand, dreaming about our next encounter. I wondered what his name was. Something strong. Nothing gender-neutral. God no. He was way too much of a man for that gender-neutral shit. Matthew. James. John. A strong biblical name. His parents probably lived in an old farmhouse in Connecticut. A property they would one day leave to us in their will. When I'm seventy, I'll be tending to my fresh lilacs, making dinner from scratch using fresh garden produce, all while drinking wine and listening to Frank Sinatra on the old record player. We'd still be madly in love after all the years together. He and I would finish off the bottle of wine, dancing the night away in our living room as...

"What the shit, Perry? Michael is waiting for the final script."

Her harsh voice cut through Frank Sinatra like her bangs cut through her forehead. I mindlessly sat up and shuffled some papers around on my desk. It was only as an adult that I started to notice my daydreams tended to interfere with actual life.

"Eddie said it would be ready in twenty minutes."

A stack of papers began to slide off the side of the desk. I smacked my hand down in an attempt to save them. Two pages stayed put, another thirty fell to the floor. Kate looked on in disgust.

"That was fucking forty-five minutes ago."

"Oh my god. What?" *Had I really spent forty-five minutes thinking about what color to paint the master bedroom in the Connecticut farmhouse?*

"For fuck's sake, Perry. Get your shit together."

Two months into the job and I liked to call Kate my friend. She liked to remind me that we were not friends, we were co-workers. *Do not call me in an emergency. I will not be there for you.* Those were her exact words the day I suggested we exchange cell phone numbers.

Kate was born and raised in Manhattan. She was a straight shooter, a little rough around the edges. Anyone who met her for the first time might categorize her as standoffish. This was the exact image she wished to portray and she did so with very calculated conversations. As hard to believe as it was, somewhere beneath the surface she was quite the hopeless romantic. She was just too insecure to own up to it. I often spent the first hour of my morning slurping coffee and listening to her dissect every minute of her date from the night before.

Me: Wait, are we talking about Tony who likes it with the lights off, Dan who went down on you for an hour, or Blake who dates women for his parents' sake, but told you he thinks he's gay, then had sex with you and confirmed he was definitely gay?

Kate: Shut the fuck up.

About a week ago, over a few beers, I had finally gotten buzzed enough to mention Ben's name. *Yeah. He's just this guy. Basically I was in love with him. But we're just friends. I'm a child. He's with someone named Dana now.* I proceeded to delve into the specifics of the night Ben and I climbed onto the roof of his car and gazed up at the stars for three hours. Two and a half hours if you factored in the thirty minutes spent hooking up.

Kate entertained my loosely strung together memories for a few minutes before promptly cutting me off. *Where is this story going? I'm too young and available to waste time listening to this. He doesn't love you, babe. He's not with you. He's with Dana.* She rested a sympathetic hand on my shoulder and chugged the rest of her Cabernet.

I went to bed that night very aware that I was lonely. No one ever warned me that the more people you jammed into a square mile radius, the lonelier you could feel. But it was real. Loneliness was there, lurking around every corner. It visited me the same time every night. *Hello Perry, it's your dear friend.*

One week to the day after our first encounter at the coffee shop, we met again. I was on my way out when I spotted him through the glass. I blushed and quickly diverted my attention at the floor. He pulled the door open and held it for me.

"So how's that mug?"

I laughed, looking up at him. The more I looked, the more I became unsure of my first impression of his eyes. They appeared lighter now. I could make out a spattering of green mixed subtly throughout. *His eyes are definitely brown and green. I think that has a name.*

"It's fantastic."

"I really like what they did with the design. Do you think they're all sold out? I would love to get one."

"You better ask. But don't touch the one on the shelf. That's a display."

He held out his hand. Mine disappeared into it. His grip was firm.

"Carter."

"Perry."

"Are you headed to work?"

"Yeah." I pointed in the direction of my building. "My office is right around the corner."

"Do you mind if I grab a coffee and walk with you?"

Every night since I moved to New York City I lay in my bed, waiting for loneliness to visit. I fixated on the street lamp outside of my window. Its bright light illuminated 51st Street. It was hypnotizing. I figured that maybe, just maybe, if I stared at that street lamp and stopped myself from drifting off to sleep, then loneliness wouldn't come. It would forget all about me. But it never forgot. It didn't matter what time it was or how long I resisted.

And then I met him. We shook hands. He walked me to work and we laughed. Our connection was natural, easy. He asked for my number and without warning I was swept up in an entirely new direction. The loneliness didn't visit that night. It didn't visit the night after. Or the night after that. It was gone.

Do not daydream on a train platform, it's dangerous

Friday, October 19, 2007, 7:53pm

I stared down the empty tunnel. All the way down to where the train tracks disappeared into the darkness. I was fairly certain that if I stared long enough I could will the train to move faster. Then, in an odd sort of way, I began to think I preferred the tunnel the way it was. The darkness was comforting. It made me feel hopeful, like the train could rip through the station at any moment and take me anywhere I wanted to go. Just for tonight. The possibilities were endless.

A man in a suit rushed down the stairs and approached the yellow line that ran along the edge of the platform. He glanced at his watch for a moment, then strained his neck to get a better view of the tunnel. His eyes appeared heavy. A long day at the office, I suppose. He was anxious to get somewhere, anywhere. *Doesn't he know we're all anxious?*

The sound of drums echoed through the underground space. I could hear the rhythmic tapping through my headphones. I turned to find a young man crouched over three buckets, all positioned upside down. His hands moved quickly over each one as a small crowd began to form around him. I looked up at the electronic board. Three minutes more until the uptown train would rattle its way down the track and shatter the darkness.

My headphones fell silent. The electronic board ticked down to two minutes. I pressed play and waited for shuffle to bring me to the next tune. The man in the suit paced back and forth. He strained his neck for a second time, frustrated once more by the looming darkness. I was growing more impatient with him. *Can't you see the fucking board? It's right above your idiot skull.*

And then his voice poured out of the headphones and into my ears, making it impossible to think about the man in the suit. It took my breath away, really. It was a voice I hadn't heard in years. A chill ran down my spine. The first verse played out. I closed my eyes and hummed along.

My mind drifted to that October night sophomore year. We were buzzed. Maybe we were borderline shitfaced if memory serves me right. I rested my head on his chest. He held my hand is his. We danced as he sang the lyrics over the melody coming out of Ali's old record player. And then we kissed. It wasn't the first time. But in that moment the feelings between us were so intense that it felt perfect. The next day Ali informed me that *someone* had taken the Otis Redding album out and placed it back in the wrong spot. It came after Otis Blackwell. Never before.

I opened my eyes now to find two headlights cutting through the darkness. It was just as the electronic board had predicted. I quickly pushed the memory from my mind. The train doors parted and I slipped into the crowded car. The train whisked me through the underground of the city, its lights flickering on and off. *It could take me anywhere.* I kept my eyes closed, letting Otis haunt me for a few moments more.

Go with your gut

If there was ever a time to poop, now was not that time. I tried my best to ignore it. I kept up a brisk pace even when it became obvious that my bowels were churning up a disaster underneath my little black dress. And when the rumbling sensation reverberated throughout my entire body, I made sure to crank the speed up to a light jog in hopes that I could simply run it off. But if one thing is this world is certain, you can't run from the truth. My hard denial caught up with me on the corner of 72nd Street and Columbus. A stabbing pain in my gut sent me toppling forward on the sidewalk in front of a boutique hotel. I rested my hands on my knees in utter agony.

"Holy shit."

A fart slithered its way through my tightly clenched cheeks. There was no denying that my underwear was now wet. *A shart right now? You are a cruel, cruel world.*

"Hey. Hey you."

He was eyeing me carefully, his hands clasped behind his back. A droplet of water trickled down my forehead. I hadn't even realized I was sweating. I was too preoccupied by the fact that there was literal shit in my underwear that could spill onto the sidewalk with even the slightest flinch in the wrong direction.

"If you're going to throw up honey, this isn't the place. Keep it moving. Let's go."

From my vantage point he appeared to be a short, stocky, rather angry looking doorman. *I'd be angry too if someone made me wear that hat.* I squinted to get a better look. He reminded me of someone. Or something for that matter. Almost like an oversized wooden nutcracker that was accidentally brought to life to terrorize the shit out of Manhattan with the rest of his evil nutcracker friends. I wasn't about to let him take over this city. Not tonight.

"Don't call me honey."

"I don't care if you want to be called Dave, just get out of my sight."

"I have menstrual cramps, dick. Thanks for the compassion."

I turned my attention back to the concrete. *Forget the fucking nutcracker. You sharted, girl. What the fuck are you going to do about it?*

"What did you call me?"

He stepped forward. The man was relentless. A savage nutcracker, who certainly didn't care that I was in the middle of a crisis.

"I called you a dick."

He scoffed, looking up and down the block to see if anyone else had heard this. He apparently had a reputation to protect in this part of town. Meanwhile, the stabbing pain suddenly returned and I clenched my stomach with both hands. My underwear would never survive another attack. It would surely fold under the pressure. I began to panic.

"Sir, please." I held my palm up towards his face. "Just back up. You have no idea."

"No. I will not back up. Do you see all of this sidewalk right here?"

He outlined a small area of pavement with his pointer fingers.

"I own it. I have hundreds of guests coming in and out of these doors all night long and I don't think they